Flight to the Promised Land

by the same author
DANGEROUS JOURNEY

Flight to the Promised Land

László Hámori

Translated from the Swedish by Annabelle MacMillan

Illustrated by Mel Silverman

Harcourt, Brace & World, Inc., New York

Contents

1	A Fantastic Awakening	9
2	The Messenger from San'a	23
3	"David Reigns in Jerusalem"	34
4	The Outwitted Robbers	41
5	The Arrival in San'a	50
6	Seeing the City	61
7	Aden, the Second Stop	71
8	In Expectation of the Miracle	81
9	On Eagles' Wings	93
10	All Our Beginnings Are Difficult	103
11	In a New World	117
12	Three Steps Forward and Two Steps Back	135
13	The Big Plan	154
14	The Genuine Adventure	169
	A Postscript	185

Flight to the Promised Land

1

A Fantastic Awakening

Shalom was hungry. It was not unusual for him to awaken feeling that way, but now there was something else, something unusual. He was aware of a sort of buzzing and of some quiet, distant music. Still half asleep, he slowly looked around.

Suddenly his eyes opened wide. He was lying, not on a mat on the floor as he did at home, but on some sort of elevation, at least half a yard above the floor. This is peculiar, he thought. How did I get here? Though he wanted to sit up, he was so weak that he could not. It was then that he noticed something strange beneath his head—something soft and white in which he could bury his face. Back home in Marib, a town in the small country of Yemen, he had never seen any such thing. There, when you went to bed, you simply folded a blanket and put it under your head.

There was no end to the curiosities here. His body and arms were covered by a snow-white garment made of thin material. In Yemen only the rulers and the very rich were able to afford such clothing. But here he lay, Shalom from Marib, on a strange sort of elevation, dressed in the clothing of the wealthy. How could this be? Cautiously he ran his fingers over the pillow and over his shirt sleeves. Never before had he seen anything so fine.

The most amazing thing of all was a beautifully carved, long, and narrow object, suspended from an iron framework in the ceiling, which slowly but ceaselessly whirled around and around, in spite of the fact that no human hand seemed to be moving it. He let his eyes follow the circular movement, expecting it to come to a halt any minute, but it continued to rotate. He was so fascinated by this puzzling phenomenon that he failed to notice someone had come alongside his bed.

"So, you're awake, are you? How do you feel, my little friend?"

The speaker was a woman, and the appearance of this woman was just as strange as everything else. Never had he seen anything like her at home in Yemen. Her face was as white as milk, her eyes were as blue as the sky, and on her head was a little white cap. And beneath the cap was a head of curly hair, as golden as ripening wheat. Neither the face nor the golden hair could really belong to a human being, Shalom mused to himself, because everybody in the world has brownish skin, black hair, and black eyes.

In his astonishment he couldn't seem to answer her.

"Don't you understand Hebrew, fellow? Why don't you answer?" the lovely vision asked amiably.

"Yes, I understand Hebrew. And I feel fine, thank you. But I'm hungry, and I can't seem to lift myself up."

Her mouth widened into a smile.

"You're a little weak, but pretty soon you'll get your strength back. Just wait and see. And soon you'll get a bite of breakfast. What's your name, anyway?"

"Shalom of the Mizrachi family. My father's name was Isaac, but he's dead. And who are you?" Shalom asked shyly.

"My name is Ingrid. I'll go now and get you some breakfast. You'll have food in a few minutes."

Ingrid walked toward the door, and as she left, Shalom could see that she, too, was dressed in white, but her dress reached only to her knees. Her legs were bare and were just as white as her face. In Yemen, all the women were dressed in loosely fitting, floor-length garments, always dark in color. If a woman were to display her bare legs the way Ingrid did, she would either be stoned or put in prison. Here, apparently, no one thought anything of such a display.

Ingrid, Shalom thought. That can't be a person's name! He had never heard of anyone named Ingrid, and furthermore he couldn't recall that the name had ever been mentioned in the Bible. At this point in his musings, Ingrid returned with a tray in hand.

"To begin with, you won't be allowed to eat very much because your stomach wouldn't be able to stand it after your long fast. Here are two sandwiches and a glass of milk. Tomorrow you'll have something more nourishing. Try to sit up now, Shalom."

Obediently, he made the effort—successfully but not without considerable strain. The bread, snow-white, light, and almost airy, was a totally new experience for him. The taste was completely different from the bread they ate at home. Moreover, this bread was much, much better. The manna that rained down from heaven when the Jews wandered in the desert must have tasted like this, Shalom decided, and began to eat. The milk was an even greater surprise than the bread. It was ice cold and as sweet as the little spoonful of honey one was given during the high holidays back home. "Not even the King of Yemen—not even the Imam himself

—could ever have anything like this milk," Shalom said to himself contentedly.

The effort of sitting up and eating had made him rather tired. Sinking back to his pillow, he closed his eyes. He had to have a little time to puzzle things out because he could understand nothing of his surroundings.

He began to recall a long journey with his mother, his sister, his brother Yussef, the schoolmaster Mori Alfeka, and the other Jews from Marib. Suddenly the lovely city of San'a appeared before his eyes, and then he began to remember how he had knocked down a soldier with a stone just as the soldier was about to rob the people of Marib. He remembered his great hunger and thirst during the journey through a stony wasteland. Gradually the whole picture grew clear in his mind, from their departure from Marib to their capture by the Bedouins. He recalled that he had gotten sick in the oasis and that he had lain there suffering, his body racked with fever.

All of a sudden he began to understand what must have happened. Of course! He had died from the fever, and now he was in heaven. It was so simple! The thought delighted him so much that he couldn't lie still in his bed. Vigorously he began to twist and turn. At once Ingrid appeared again.

"What's the matter, Shalom? Don't you feel well?"

"Oh, yes. Blessed be the Lord. But can I ask you a question?"

"Certainly you may. Ask as many questions as you want."

"Well, there's just one thing. Are you an angel, Ingrid?"

Ingrid's answer came in the form of resounding laughter.

"Go to sleep now, Shalom. Later this afternoon we can talk some more. I'll have more time then. Right now I have to see to it that the others get their breakfast," she said as she left him.

The boy's eyes followed the figure in white until her almost noiseless steps carried her through the door. Very appropriate for an angel to walk so silently. After that he began to stare again at the narrow moving object that slowly, majestically, rotated from the ceiling with a soft, buzzing sound. This made him sleepy, and soon he closed his eyes again. He felt happy and contented, and just as he was about to fall asleep, he decided that the elderly schoolmaster Mori Alfeka was right—right when he said that the people who observed the laws of their religion would be rewarded, after death, in the heavenly kingdom, would live among the heavenly host in everlasting bliss.

It's a good thing that I studied so hard on my lessons and that I obeyed Mori Alfeka and my brother Yussef, he thought, although the matter of obeying his brother had perhaps been a little questionable every now and then, he had to admit. But now it doesn't make any difference, because I got to heaven in any case, and Ingrid the angel gives me cold milk to drink and snow-white bread to eat.

Sighing happily, he fell asleep. He awoke to hear Ingrid saying, "Yes, the boy regained consciousness this morning, and his appetite seemed good. His fever is down."

Her words were addressed to another figure in white, but in spite of the white garment, this new figure wasn't a bit like Ingrid. He was half a head taller, and there was no white cap on his head. Instead there was only a bald pate that glistened like the copper kettles back home after Shalom's mother had scoured them on Friday afternoons. He had scarcely any hair left except for a couple of graying tufts at his temples. However, the most interesting thing about him was the two small panes of glass sitting in front of his eyes. His face was wrinkled. The panes of glass were framed in gold. Never before had Shalom seen a bare-headed man, and certainly not one who had windows in front of his eyes.

"Naturally, that's because he is an angel. Of course, they have to look different," he said to himself.

"How do you feel now, boy?" the bald angel asked.

"Thank you, reverend sir, I feel well, thanks be to God," Shalom answered respectfully.

"I'm glad to hear it. I guess the boy can have a little more food and some vitamin pills now, Ingrid. And he can get up tomorrow morning."

Whereupon Ingrid and the bald angel left his bedside. Shalom's eyes followed the two figures in white. To his surprise, he discovered that there were three other strange elevations, similar to the one on which he lay, in the room. There were people on all three of them. On the nearest of them lay an old, bearded Yemenite in a blue turban. Ingrid and the other figure in white stopped at his bedside. Ingrid explained something to her escort, but though she spoke in Hebrew, Shalom couldn't understand a word she said. He watched the bald angel lift up the Yemenite's arm and stick some sort of nail, which, in turn, was fastened to a small bottle, into his dark brown skin. The man in the turban muttered something and swore under his breath. Unmistakably he swore!

The bald angel handed the needle back to Ingrid, and they continued on to both the other elevations that stood farther away in the corner of the room.

The scene that Shalom had just witnessed caused him to have mixed feelings. In place of calm content came the same intense curiosity that had filled him ever since they had left Marib. While he puzzled over what he had just seen, Ingrid and her companion left the room. Shalom turned to the old man on the nearest elevation.

"Blessings on you, sir, and peace be with you," he said with respect.

"The same to you," said the man in the blue turban in a none too friendly voice.

"Sir, why did you just swear? The angels don't like it very much if you swear in heaven, do they?"

"You're an absolute fool," the old man said angrily as he turned his back—an obvious signal that he didn't wish to continue the conversation. All Shalom could see was his black hair peeping out from the middle of the turban.

"That's odd," Shalom said to himself. "If he has lived a sufficiently God-fearing life that he could get to heaven, I wonder how he can behave in such an unmannerly fashion once he's here?"

The old man, however, seemed to have regretted his action and soon turned over again, facing Shalom. Without giving the boy time to pose any further questions, he began to speak in a high, whining voice. The words flowed from him—a rather uncommon thing with most Yemenites.

"What's this nonsense about angels and heaven, boy? I think hell would be preferable. Just be on your guard. . . . Angels! Those people dressed in white? No! Just the opposite! Do you know what they do to me? They come here every day and stick needles into me. In the beginning they stuck me in the thigh, but now they've started with my arms. It hurts so much afterwards that I can hardly move. And have you seen what they look like? A woman with bare legs and a man who goes around with his head uncovered—a man who has shaved off his beard. They are Jews, and they speak Hebrew, but they have rejected the laws of their religion. When I think that I had to land in a place like this. . . . Ach, if only I had never left Yemen and had stayed in my own workshop instead! We have been deceived by false prophets. Somebody convinced us falsely that the land of Israel has arisen again and that we'll be able to live in peace and gladness there. And instead they torment good, orthodox Jews by sticking needles in them."

The outburst left the old man so feeble that he began to pant.

His eyes, wrinkled at the corners, closed, and he lay motionless upon his elevation as if he had suddenly fallen asleep or fainted. With fear and trembling, Shalom observed him, not daring to say a word. For a while the silence in the room was broken only by the rotary movement of the object in the ceiling. All the while it whirred with a faint sound. Suddenly Shalom heard Ingrid's voice again.

"What's on your mind now, Shalom? Sit up, because here comes your noon meal. Eat it all up so you'll be healthy and strong again."

Ingrid placed a tray of food before him. On the tray was a white bowl with some sort of white food in it, and alongside the bowl was a gleaming spoon. Beside the spoon stood a huge glass of cold milk. Eagerly Shalom began to eat, finding that the white porridge tasted very good indeed. It was as sweet as if it had been cooked in honey, and it was better than anything Mother used to fix for the high holidays in Marib. "I'm sure this is what they call manna from heaven," Shalom said to himself.

"That's a good boy, Shalom," Ingrid said, praising him when she saw that both the bowl and the glass were empty.

"If you keep this up, you can go back to your own people in just a few days."

"Are . . . are they dead too?" asked Shalom in alarm.

"What makes you think they're dead?" Ingrid replied. "They're alive and healthy. I just told you that you can go back to them in a few days. But I don't have time to stand here talking to you now. The other people have to have their food too."

Shalom understood even less than before. If his brother and mother and sister weren't dead and if he were going to join them in just a few days, perhaps he wasn't dead himself, either. Or was it possible that he was dead but that he was going to be restored to life? Perhaps they didn't want him in heaven because he had squabbled with both his brother and his schoolmaster from time to time. And when he had knocked down the askari—the soldier—with the stone, he had been disobedient to Mori Alfeka. But then if he weren't worthy of remaining in paradise, why did Ingrid feed him all that wonderful manna? Or could it be that the man in the blue turban was right? All that afternoon he lay there twisting and turning uneasily in his bed. At length he summoned up courage to ask his neighbor in the turban, but then he saw that the old man was sitting up and praying. Naturally he couldn't disturb him at that moment. Rocking the upper part of his body rhythmically back and forth, the old man finally sank back to his pillow and went to sleep immediately. Regularly spaced snores emerged from his beard, the noise blending with the whirring sound coming from the ceiling.

Meanwhile, twilight had come, and soon it was totally dark in the room. No longer could Shalom control his apprehensiveness. Hastily he shot up out of bed. The most difficult thing was to get his feet out from under the covers, but finally he managed to set them on the floor. The exertion made him a little dizzy, and in the beginning his legs didn't really do what he wanted them to, but soon he was able to walk. He went in the direction of the door through which Ingrid had disappeared. A nicely shaped knob glistened on the door, and Shalom tried to pull it to one side as he had always done with the wooden locks in Yemen. The lock, however, would not move. But once he had pushed down on the lock, the door opened. He didn't have time to be surprised about this because just on the other side of the door he encountered the next miracle. A brilliant light filled the small room, even though he could see neither a tallow candle nor an oil lamp. And in the middle of the room sat Ingrid at a little white table.

In a minute Shalom noticed that the light came from a little glass object that hung by a string from the ceiling. When Ingrid caught sight of the boy in the door, she cried in alarm.

"For heaven's sake, Shalom. . . . What has happened? Are you sick? Why did you get up?"

"There's nothing wrong, respected Ingrid. But I am simply taking the opportunity to ask you a number of things. You promised me this morning that you would talk to me when you had time . . ."

"Come and sit down here, then, Shalom, so that we can talk. I do have a little more time now. Do you want some milk?" Without waiting for his response, she went over to a white cabinet in the corner, took out a glass container, and poured out a glass of milk. Shalom lifted it to his lips, and

—what a miracle!—the milk was so cold that he almost shivered.

"How can the milk be so cold?" he asked, almost frightened. "Even when we let the milk stand in the cellar, it was never this cold at home."

"This is a refrigerator. It runs by electricity, and it keeps food cold," Ingrid explained.

"Elec . . . electricity? What's that, anyway?"

"Oh, I forgot. Probably you people from down there in Marib have never once seen ice. Come and I'll show you what it looks like." Ingrid opened the door of the white cabinet, took out a tray, and let an ice cube fall into Shalom's hand. With wide-open eyes, he stared at the ice cube glistening in the light.

"It's like the crystal that the jewelers use to make expensive ornaments for the *shereef*. May I have it?"

"Of course!" Ingrid laughed. "But I'm afraid you won't have very much long-lasting joy from that present. Now sit down, Shalom," she said, pointing to a chair.

"I can't sit on anything like that," the boy said almost in shame. "In Yemen we sit on mats on the floor—like this." And he crouched down, supporting his back with his heels.

"Well, sit any way you like if you think it's more comfortable," Ingrid said. "In good time you'll get to Israel, and there you can learn to sit on a chair. What was it you wanted to ask me about?"

Shalom, however, said nothing. He merely stared at his hand. Water had already begun to drop from it. The glistening piece of ice became smaller and smaller with every passing second. He began to understand why Ingrid had told him that the pleasure he would have from her present would be short-lived. The sight of that beautiful crystal

simply disappearing before his eyes made him very sad, and
tears began to stream from his large black eyes. At length
he regained his composure and dried his wet hand on his
nightshirt.

"Will you be good enough to tell me if you and the man
with the windows in front of his eyes are angels or not?"

"Neither of us is an angel," Ingrid replied with a smile.
"We are people just like yourself and like the old man there
beside you. The doctor and I, as well as fifty other people,
have come here to the settlement to help the refugees from
Yemen."

Her explanation was disappointing to Shalom. If Ingrid
and the person she referred to as the doctor weren't angels,
then this couldn't be paradise. But what about all the
miracles, then—light without lamps or candles, crystal that
melted, an object that whirred about in the ceiling, manna
made with honey, and everything else? And above all, how
could Ingrid have golden hair?

"All these things which seem so odd to you aren't miracles
at all," Ingrid continued. "They are just examples of technical progress. Where you lived in Yemen, everything has
stood still for three hundred years or more. That's why you
don't know about electricity, fans, eyeglasses, and many
other discoveries. But in Israel, you'll learn to know about
all these things."

"But why is your hair so golden?"

"Well, that's because I came to Israel from Sweden, you
see. Up in the far north there are many people who have
hair the same color as mine. There's nothing peculiar about
that, Shalom."

"Sweden?" Shalom had never heard of that country. At
home in Marib he knew about Saudi Arabia, Hadhramaut,

and Aden, as well as all the countries whose names appear in the Bible. But the Scriptures had never even mentioned Sweden. I guess I'll learn about that in Israel, Shalom thought.

"But, dear Ingrid, please explain to me where I am and how I got here. And tell me, too, why you stick nails in the old man beside me if you have come here from Israel to help the Jews who came from Yemen."

"This is the El Hasched settlement, Shalom, not far from Aden. And this is the settlement's hospital. You were sent here to the hospital from the territory run by the Sultan of Kuri. Many of you were sick, and you have come here to get well. The other people live in the settlement. We aren't sticking nails into the old man; we're giving him injections. The doctor is putting medicine into his arteries. Don't you understand?"

"Not really," Shalom admitted. "If a sick person back home in Marib doesn't get better with prayers said for him, our surgeon puts hot, glowing nails on the place where his pain is in order to drive out the evil spirits. It seems you do things in a different way here. But tell me, Ingrid, how long am I going to stay here? When can I go back to my family? And why are we in this particular settlement?"

Patiently Ingrid explained to Shalom that he would be able to leave the hospital as soon as he could regain his strength, but before that he would have to get a lot of sleep and eat a lot of nourishing food. She added that all the people who were living in the El Hasched settlement were waiting to get to Israel, where they would begin a new life.

"And when are we going to go there? And how?"

"I can't answer that at the moment," Ingrid said sadly.

"There are a good many people besides yourself who are wondering about that. But with God's help, I'm sure we'll come up with a solution, and you'll soon all be able to go to Israel together."

2

The Messenger from San'a

Shalom belonged to a family who for many generations had worked as silversmiths—a family well known in the town of Marib and among the Bedouins in the desert, which spreads out to the east of Marib, for the beautiful and durable inlaid silverwork they did.

Shalom expected to continue in his father's well-trod footsteps, to learn the art of silver inlays and to work in the family workshop. But something drastic and unexpected happened.

Early one sun-drenched morning in May, the buyers and sellers assembled in the large square outside Marib for the regular monthly bazaar. The town itself lay at the crest of the slope of a rather long hill, while the open market was about a half hour's journey from the town, down on the flatlands. During the rainy season, uncontrolled streams of water rushed along a deep ravine, right up to the market square, but in the summertime there were only small pools left from the heavy floods. From these pools, the camels, mules, and horses that belonged to the market people eagerly lapped up the muddy drops of water.

Yussef Mizrachi, Shalom's older brother, was arranging his handmade silver articles on a handwoven piece of tapestry. Shalom helped him by placing three pistols in a row on the striped mat—three pistols of a simple sort that had been decorated with silver inlay. The cost of these was one sheep each in payment.

When a Bedouin boy reaches manhood, he receives a pistol from his father. The weapon is placed in his broad waist belt, and it serves as a sign that the boy is now fully grown.

At this point the young Bedouin has his own flock of sheep and goes to live in his own tent with his own wives. But the pistol is not really his until it has been embellished with a silver-inlaid pattern of his choosing. For this reason, he goes to the market place in Marib and leaves it with the silversmith after much haggling over the pattern and the price of the work.

It can take up to two months before the work is finished —perhaps longer if the owner has decided upon an especially elegant and complicated pattern. For this special sort of craftsmanship he might have to give as payment four sheep in good condition, or twelve sheepskins.

The Mizrachi brothers had just finished readying their stall when a man appeared, running along the sloping road from the city. Very seldom do you see a grown man running in Yemen. In the first place, their ground-length clothing doesn't lend itself to racing, and furthermore, since ancient times it has been felt that the dignity of an adult demands that he move slowly and talk very sparingly. "Only slaves and persons being pursued stoop to running," an old Yemenite proverb explains.

But the man who was running down the slope gave not a thought, obviously, to his dignity. Hoisting his garment as high as he could, he progressed as fast as his bare legs could carry him. Shalom noticed at once that he was not an Arab but a Jew, because he didn't have the usual broad Arab belt around his middle.

The man soon reached the market place and hurried up to one of the sandalmakers, exchanging a number of words with him. Then he continued on to another seller, and thus, in turn, spoke with all the Jewish merchants. Eventually he came to Yussef as well, but Shalom did not catch what the messenger whispered in his brother's ear. He saw only that his brother nodded his head three times and said "ken, ken, ken" a like number of times, which indicates that you are in agreement with the speaker.

Immediately the messenger rushed on to another merchant, and Shalom, filled with curiosity, eyed his brother in the hope that he would be told what it was all about. Since the death of their father two years before, Yussef had been the head of the Mizrachi family. Though he was no more than twenty years old, it was Shalom's duty to obey and honor him as the head of the family.

Any family member not yet thirteen years of age who dared to pose a question to the head of the family might be rewarded by being boxed on the ears. No matter how curious Shalom was, he didn't want to risk anything like that.

Yussef didn't look once at Shalom. Several times he ran his fingers through his beard, which in the whole of the land of Yemen is an unfailing sign that a person is deep in thought. Then he placed the precious inlaid articles back into their protective linen cases. Only the three simply decorated pistols and a few small brooches and cheap silver chains were left in view on the woven mat.

"Listen to me, Shalom. I have to go back to the city. Stay here and sell what you can. You know the prices. The

owners will almost surely come for their pistols, but if they
aren't here by noon, pack everything up and come home.
God grant His help to you, and peace be with you!"

The boy listened intently; his eyes were opened wide. He
couldn't imagine what had happened to make Yussef decide
to leave the market place before the day's business had even
begun. He took considerable pride in the fact that his
brother dared to trust him with all the expensive things, in
spite of the fact that he hadn't had his thirteenth birthday
and that he had not finished school. But his pride was mixed
with uneasiness and, above all, with tremendous curiosity.

Shalom's anxiety and wonder began to mount when he
noticed that it wasn't only Yussef who was leaving the
market place but also all the other Jewish merchants. Some
of them entrusted their wares to a son or a younger brother,
but most of them packed up their merchandise and trudged
along toward town with their sacks on their backs.

Shalom didn't have much time for contemplation because soon the customers began to appear. Most of them
were Bedouins so completely shrouded by their blue
burnooses that you could only catch a glimpse of their eyes
at the top and their sandals at the bottom. Burnooses are
made of linen dyed with indigo, so that they soil less easily
and don't have to be washed so often as if they were white.
The desert people might have seemed rather frightening in
their blue garments with their pistols and their wide, curved
daggers hanging from their belts, but Shalom wasn't afraid.
He had been used to them since childhood and knew that,
all things considered, they were fine, honorable people, even
if they regarded petty thievery as no special crime.

Thanks to Shalom's watchfulness, not a single silver
article disappeared from the striped mat. As he bargained

with the Bedouins, he tried to mimic the tone of voice he
had so often heard his brother Yussef use. But no matter
how he tried, no one bought anything. The customers merely
continued along to some other silversmith's display. The
only thing he managed to sell that whole morning was a
small brooch.

Shalom found it difficult to concentrate on the business
matters at hand. He was still puzzled as to why the heads
of the families had been summoned back to the city.

Something very unusual must have happened. But what?

The three Bedouins with the special orders all came in
their turn to collect their pistols. Before paying, they inspected the butts of the pistols. One of them even took out
his curved dagger—a jambia, as it is called—from its
sheath in order to tell, by using its point, whether or not
the silver inlay was fastened tightly enough into the wood
so as not to come loose in time. But none of these suspicious
Bedouins could find any fault in the work of the Mizrachis.

Shalom collected the payments agreed upon. Even though
desert people can easily steal some little thing if you aren't
on your guard, the Bedouins feel that it is a dishonor and a
disgrace not to stand by your word. Two of the pistol
owners paid with one sheep each, which Shalom examined
as scrupulously as they had examined their pistols. He
looked at their teeth to ascertain that they weren't too old,
after which he ran his hands through the curly hair of their
hides to establish that no defects were to be found. Such
defects were caused by fungus growths or insect bites, and
they, in turn, produced bumps about the size of a fingertip.
Tanners did not pay much for damaged hides.

The third Bedouin paid, not with a sheep, but with cash.
Into the boy's outstretched hand he counted out three huge,

round silver rials, which he had taken from his pouch. Shalom knew what condition the coins should be in, so he bit into each one of them. Counterfeit money is abundant in all parts of the world. Shalom had learned that you have to examine coins carefully before accepting them. If they are of genuine silver, you can see no teeth marks, but if they are counterfeit pieces made out of lead or zinc, the teeth marks remain on the coin.

Later, when there were no customers in front of his display, Shalom took out the three silver coins and inspected them once again carefully. Not often in his life had he held real money in his hands, to say nothing of a coin worth as much as a rial.

On one side was the bust of a plump, awe-inspiring lady, and this was surrounded by letters of a strange alphabet— neither Hebrew nor Arabic. On the other side was an image of a strange, but beautiful, two-headed bird with outstretched wings.

The coin was a Maria Theresa dollar, named for the ruler of Austria-Hungary—the lady whose bust was on the other side of the coin. The empress had permitted these coins to be minted in Vienna about 1780, and via Ethiopia they had passed through many hands until they had reached the Arabic countries.

These Oriental people must have been fond of the picture of this high-bosomed empress, for long after the coin was no longer in use in the country of its origin, it was still used as currency in both Yemen and Saudi Arabia. The mint in Vienna still made them at the order of the Arabic sovereigns. The Maria Theresa dollar is called a rial in Yemen.

Suddenly from the city could be heard a number of long-drawn-out howls of lament: they were the cries from the mosque. It was the muezzin who, from the circular terrace on the tower, announced the Mohammedan creed:

"Allah is one God and Mohammed is his prophet."

Three times the cry was repeated from the minaret as a signal that it was time for the midday prayers.

In accordance with the Mohammedan Scriptures, the Bedouins and Arabian buyers hurried to the ravine to dip their fingers in the water and anoint their eyes and their foreheads. In no time at all the market place was full of men, kneeling on their prayer rugs, bowing their turban or burnoose-covered heads in the direction of their holy city, Mecca. There in the blazing sun they repeated their prayers.

Meanwhile, the Jewish merchants had packed up their remaining stock, lashed together the sheep they had received in payment, and were slowly making their way up to the city again. Shalom joined the crowd with his small pack on his shoulder and two woolly sheep in front of him.

Marib lies almost in the middle of the country of Yemen, toward its eastern border. The town is situated at the foot of a mighty range of mountains, right where the mountains meet the desert.

The entire city consists of some hundred or more houses and a citadel. In the citadel lived the province's mighty ruler, the Emir, with his wives, his children, and his bodyguard of thirty soldiers.

Shalom's family lived right at the edge of the town on the winding Street of the Jews. All the Jewish families in Marib lived on the same street, but not because they were fond of living at the edge of the city. It was because they were not permitted to live anywhere else, and they were forced to content themselves with houses which were lower than any other buildings in the city.

Shalom's uncontrollable curiosity lent wings to his feet, and not even the boiling midday sun could check his eagerness to get home as quickly as possible. He was too eager to find out why the messenger had summoned his brother Yussef and the others from the market place.

Now and then he hit the sheep with the end of the rope in order to get them to hurry, and he was the first one to reach his home on the Street of the Jews. He drove the sheep through the gate leading to the family's cube-shaped house and locked them in a stall to the right.

The workshop took up the left half of the house and opened out onto the sandy street. As had his father, grandfather, and forefathers for several centuries back, Yussef usually sat inside, squatting on a homemade woven mat, about halfway out to the street, working at his craft with a trained hand and a sure eye. Inside the workshop itself, where light from the street seldom reached, there was nothing but the huge, ancient cupboard.

But today Yussef was not to be found in the workshop. Shalom hurried along the corridor leading to the back part of the house, where the kitchen was located. There sat his mother and sister on the kitchen floor grinding corn in a mill consisting of two shiny stones, worn by years of hard use. Above the open fireplace, which stood encircled by stones in the middle of the kitchen, burned sheep tallow, which filled the large room with its heavy smell.

"Peace be unto you, Mother. Peace be with you, Sister! Where did Yussef go, anyway?"

"Welcome, my son! We haven't seen Yussef since you both took off for the market place this morning. But the

neighbor's wife was here about an hour ago, and she told
us that her husband had come back from the market along
with Yussef and the heads of the other families. But she
didn't know why."

Mother continued her account, but to deaf ears, because
Shalom immediately ran out into the street again and
headed straight for Mori Alfeka's house. Mori Alfeka was
the philosopher and sage of the Marib Jews, the one to
whom they all turned when they needed advice, the one who
saw to it that the Scriptural laws were observed at births,
marriages, and burial ceremonies, and who, if necessary,
dealt with the Cadi, the mayor of the city, or the Emir, the
province's governor under the country's supreme ruler, the
Imam.

Mori Alfeka lived right beside the synagogue—a building that was used not only as a place for religious services
but also as a school and a meeting house for the little Jewish
community. He was a widower and lived alone in his small
house. Now, however, the house was empty, and the fire
had gone out on the hearth. The old man must have left
quite a while ago, Shalom decided. Shalom was not permitted to go inside the synagogue. There, guarding the
door, was the same man who that morning had come rushing down to the market place, all out of breath, to summon
the men. His name was Said, and he seemed to be a bit up-
set. He was neither stupid nor crazy; he was enormously
talkative. He was fond of talking and laughing to himself,
even when there was no one to hear him. He had no job,
but to keep him occupied, the Jews had made him a kind of
errand boy for Mori Alfeka.

Highly conscious of his own importance, he stopped
Shalom from entering the synagogue.

"Stop right there, Shalom! Mori Alfeka said that I can't let anyone go in, and I'm not going to let anyone in."

"Oh, well, that's all right, Uncle Said. I didn't intend to go in. But do tell me what they're up to in there."

"That's a secret, Shalom! A great big secret. But lean over this way, and I'll whisper in your ear. This morning Mori Alfeka told me to go down to the market and call the men here, and that was exactly what I did."

"You're not telling me a thing I don't know already, Uncle Said. I was there when you came. But why did Mori Alfeka call all the men here?"

The old fellow scratched himself on the neck and then replied cheerlessly, "Look here, Shalom. I don't really know. I only know that this morning a messenger arrived from the capital, from San'a. He was both dusty and tired after his journey, and when he caught sight of Mori Alfeka, he simply said, 'The rumors are true!' Whereupon Mori Alfeka kissed him on both cheeks and responded, 'Eternal God be praised!' "

3

"David Reigns in Jerusalem"

As a result of his conversation with Said, Shalom was none the wiser. "The rumors are true!" But what rumors? And why were the men called away from the market place? And what were these long deliberations in the synagogue all about? Not even when the doors of the synagogue opened for evening prayer did he manage to get an answer to his questions. The services that evening were precisely as they were on any other evening, with the two long wax candles burning up in front of the congregation, just as they always had. The only unusual thing was that a stranger sat on the low bench along the wall, right beside Mori Alfeka. But Shalom could sense the strange tension that filled the atmosphere.

Not even after evening prayer did Yussef come home to supper. Instead a message was delivered by old Said.

"Yussef said to tell you that he would be eating supper with Mori Alfeka. He wants me to bring him his food and a container of wine. I have already picked up food from four other households," the old man added, his face beaming.

Shalom's mother put out the fire in the kitchen and the oil lamps in the next room, but Shalom sat in the dark trying to figure out the strange, unusual events of the day.

He must have fallen asleep in the middle of his contemplation, however, because he never heard his brother come home.

The next day, as usual, Shalom and his brother went together to morning prayer, but Yussef didn't say a word to him during the short journey. When the prayers were over, the children remained in the synagogue and, under the leadership of Mori Alfeka, they began their lessons. But that day the elderly teacher did not take down the huge Hebrew book that contained the Holy Scriptures and that the children from Marib's Street of the Jews had used as a reader for over a century. Instead from his wide sleeve he took out his little silver box and, with two fingers, put a pinch of snuff in each nostril. For a long while after that he stroked his white beard, and for an even longer time he rolled the long curl that hung down over his ear around one of his index fingers. The boys, in a mood of great expectation, observed, with nine pairs of eager eyes, every movement of their teacher until he at last began to speak. His voice was heavy and guttural.

"Shalom, my son, tell me what it says in the Holy Scriptures about the coming of the Messiah."

" 'When the Lord our God decides that the Jews have suffered sufficiently, He will send the Messiah to deliver them from their bondage and lead them back to Israel.' That's what the prophet Isaiah says."

"Absolutely right, Shalom. That's what it says in the Scriptures. And now I want you to listen carefully to what I am about to say so that some day you'll be able to pass on the story to your children and your grandchildren."

In order to lend more emphasis to his words, old Mori Alfeka spoke to the children, not in Arabic, but in Hebrew,

the language of the Bible, and, in addition, his method of
expression was strongly reminiscent of Biblical language.
His speech was sprinkled with quotations from the holy
books, and he referred over and over to the Lord God and
His will. He told the children of the many tribulations the
Jews had been forced to live through for close to two thousand years—ever since the Roman legions of the Emperors
Vespasianus and Titus attacked the Jewish state and destroyed the kingdom of Jerusalem. Mori Alfeka had never
been further than the countryside around Marib, he had
never read anything but the Hebrew volumes containing the
Holy Scriptures, he hadn't the slightest notion of the progress of technology, and he knew virtually nothing about anything beyond the hills of Marib. He knew only how it was
for the Jews in Yemen and how they were treated as if they
had the plague. No Jew was permitted even to touch a
devout Mohammedan Yemenite, let alone take him by the
hand. No Jew could ever enter into Mohammedan houses,
and it was completely out of the question to think that an
Arab would set foot in a Jewish dwelling. If a Jew met a
Yemenite on the street, the Jew was forced to step out into
the roadway in order to make room for the devout Mohammedan. The Jews were denied the privilege of riding
either horses or camels because the Jews could not put
themselves at eye level with the disciples of the prophet
Mohammed. The Imam, who was the country's supreme
ruler, demanded twice as much tax from the Jews as from
the Arabs, and a Jew had no rights versus a Mohammedan
in the Imam's court of justice.

"And why do our forefathers and we ourselves have to
suffer all these things? Simply because we have held fast
to the belief of our forefathers and to the laws that are

spelled out in the Holy Scriptures. We are just as good as all the other people in Yemen, but they have no use for our established way of worshiping the same God whom they themselves honor," the elderly teacher said sorrowfully.

For a moment he stopped speaking and then continued with a triumphant ring to his voice.

"The humiliations and sufferings are about to come to an end. The Jews' own state, Israel, has arisen again after two thousand years, and once more a David reigns in Jerusalem, King David's city. Boys, let us praise our God that we have been privileged to experience this day and that He has granted us the mercy to return to Israel, the land of Abraham, Isaac, and of our forefathers."

Straightening his back, the old man began to intone, in a quaking voice, the ancient hymn of thanksgiving that King David, the great psalm writer, had one time composed in gratitude to God for victory.

Following the example of their teacher, the nine thin, dark-skinned boys joined in the singing of the psalm. Shalom, however, was thinking not of the beautiful text but of totally unrelated things. And the moment the elderly Alfeka sat down on his long bench again, a flood of questions issued from the mouth of Shalom.

"Tell me, honored teacher, how we know that King David reigns again over Jerusalem and that we will be allowed to return to Israel."

"Some months ago we got word that the war had begun in Israel. The rulers of all the Arabian countries sent their mighty armies against the Jews who had moved back there. Only a miracle could save them. And the miracle happened!"

"What was it that happened?"

"With God's help the Jews put one after the other of the Arabian legions out of commission. There were ten, maybe twenty, foreign soldiers, all armed to the teeth, for every Jew, but still the Jews won."

"And tell me, revered teacher Alfeka, how is it that we know all this? Israel is a long way from here."

"There is a new discovery that is called radio. Our governor, the Emir, has forbidden all radios under penalty of death, but a certain Jew in San'a has broken the governor's law and got hold of one."

"My father has also heard a radio," one of the boys cried out. "When he was in San'a, he was able to both see and hear one. He says that it is truly a great wonder."

"Because of what I just told you, we asked one of our friends—a merchant who lives in San'a but who usually comes here every month to sell salt—to tell us each time how the war in Israel was progressing. And every time our friend came to Marib, he would look me up in the evening and tell me what I wanted to know," the old man continued. "But I guarded the secret and never told anyone anything, since I didn't wish to stir up any false hopes."

"And now the hopes aren't false any longer?" Shalom asked.

"No. Now we know for certain. A free Jewish state has been proclaimed in Jerusalem, the Holy City, and the David now reigning in Israel has announced that Jews from anywhere in the world may find a home in Israel."

"Then was that the message that arrived yesterday, honorable teacher?"

"Yes, and there's even more. The leader of the Jews in San'a, the learned and respected Rabbi Halevy, blessed be his name, has gone to see the ruler of the land, the Imam,

and asked permission for the Jews in Yemen to return to the Holy Land."

"And what did the Imam say?" asked four boys simultaneously.

Smilingly, Mori Alfeka waited until they had calmed down a bit, and then said, slowly and clearly, "In the beginning the Imam was very hardhearted. But our learned Rabbi Halevy took his Torah and read to him the chapter about the ten plagues in Egypt. He had scarcely finished reading the chapter before a servant came rushing into the throne room. Terror was in his voice as he told the Imam that his favorite son, the little Prince Abdurman, had broken out all over his body. Immediately the Imam's pride disappeared. He took the fact that his favorite son was sick as a sign from God. At once he called his scribe, and he gave Rabbi Halevy a letter of safe conduct, allowing the Jews to leave the land freely. He wrote as well a letter to the governor of the province, saying that he must not in any way hinder the departure of the Jews."

"Then we can go to Israel?" Shalom asked breathlessly.

"Yes, our God be praised. . . . The messenger from the capital carried with him the Imam's letter to the Emir of Marib when he arrived here yesterday. And I'm expecting the Emir to call me to the citadel any minute."

Scarcely had Mori Alfeka said these words than the old watchman entered the synagogue.

"Mori Alfeka! Mori Alfeka! A servant of the Emir is outside. Hurry up. Come at once. The servant tells me that the Emir, the man of the shining presence, his excellency, wants to speak with you. Right away, Mori Alfeka."

Most assuredly it was the day of wonders in Marib.

4

The Outwitted Robbers

The caravan, which made its way along the winding path through the rocky mountains, consisted of twenty families, an equal number of mules, and two Yemenite soldiers. They broke camp every morning as soon as the first rays of sun were visible in the east and continued their journey, often on dangerously steep mountain paths, until about noontime. To be sure, the heat up in the high mountains was far less oppressive and unbearable than that in Marib, at the edge of the desert, but they rested during the midday hours in any case because this was their custom in that country.

There were no roads over the mountains—only paths that had been made by camel or mule caravans. The Imam didn't permit the building of roads. Roads would have to be built by foreign engineers, and he wanted none of these in his land. Furthermore, what good would roads serve? At most there were six automobiles in the whole country, and three of them belonged to the Imam himself, who never traveled anywhere. And of course even the wealthiest Yemenites did not buy automobiles—simply because there were no roads. And so, slowly but surely the heavily loaded mules made their way along the steep mountain paths.

The Emir had indeed summoned Mori Alfeka in order to haggle over the exodus of the Jews. There was great

bargaining, with stubbornness on the part of both the ruler
of the province and the leader of the Jews, because the Emir,
in accordance with ancient oriental custom, wanted to
make a bit of money out of the maneuver. The Imam's order
had said that the Jews could take with them all the personal possessions they were able to handle. The Emir did
not dare make any changes in the order itself—how could
he oppose the command of his supreme and gracious
master?—but he explained to Mori Alfeka that no family
would be allowed to take more than one mule.

The Jews in Marib had no great wealth of earthly possessions, but once they had loaded onto the mules their Holy
Scriptures, the hand-loomed wool blankets on which they
slept, and their sheepskin water canteens, there wasn't room
for much more. A few pots and pans for preparing food,
several articles of clothing, and the caravan could take no
more.

For the price of fifty rials, the Emir had detailed to them
two soldiers armed with old, long-barreled shotguns—the
Yemenites call these soldiers askari—to go along and protect the emigrants on their journey. In the mountains of
Yemen it is not unusual to find bands of robbers who attack
and rob peaceful travelers, and it was for this reason that
Mori Alfeka had hired the armed escorts from the Emir.
One of the askari led the procession, and the other one
brought up the rear. They wore no uniforms. The weapons
they carried and the cartridge belts crossed over their chests
marked them as soldiers.

The trip over the mountains was time-consuming and
tedious—at least Shalom thought so. For three days they
had been on their way, and at least a five-day journey lay
before them before they could reach San'a, the capital.

Never before had Shalom been outside of Marib, and during the preparations for the long trip, he had rushed around wildly. He didn't know what he expected of the journey, but he had been smitten by travel fever. However, apart from the feeling of tense expectation, he took no particular delight in the entire series of miraculous events—from the arrival of the messenger to Mori Alfeka's description of the preparations for their departure. But at night, after the campfire had gone out and everyone lay wrapped up in striped blankets, Shalom sat for a long time thinking. It was truly wonderful, and a great blessing from God, that the Jews, after two thousand years and during Shalom's lifetime, were being allowed by God to return to their Holy Land. But—Shalom mused in the darkness—what is it going to be like to live in Israel? It had been very nice in Marib—at least that was Shalom's opinion. True, Yussef had become impossibly demanding after the death of their father—even worse than a venerable, white-bearded old man. On occasion he had even hit Shalom when the latter hadn't obeyed his commands quickly enough, but Shalom's father had done so too, though not so often. But if Yussef was somewhat trying at times as the head of the family, Mori Alfeka, as a result, became the more respected and loved. Shalom was the best of the old man's nine pupils. He was the first to commit to memory the portion of Scripture for the day. Once they had all repeated the passage three times together, he could always repeat it alone the fourth time with no prompting from Alfeka. And if you were to ask him where this or that could be found in the Torah, he could almost immediately give the correct answer.

In school, their only reading matter was the Torah, which is the Old Testament; this they read from the ancient, heavy volume, the only book the school owned, because the Imam did not allow the importing of books from other countries, and there were neither Arabic nor Hebraic printing firms in Yemen. In the Jewish school in Marib, Mori Alfeka sat in front of the low ledge on which the book lay open, with the boys in a semicircle around him. And when he pointed at a certain boy, that boy began to read from the book. There were only boys in the school. Girls did not go to school or learn to read.

Mori Alfeka had great understanding and appreciation of Shalom's gifts. Though he seldom praised him, he showed his regard quite obviously by calling him for an hour of special study before evening prayers. During these periods, the old man taught Shalom to write with a lead pencil, not only in Hebrew but also in Arabic. The holy laws demand that every Jew must be able to read the Holy Scriptures, but no ability to write is demanded. In Yemen, any person who could write was regarded as an educated man, be he Jew or Arab.

Shalom could easily have hoped to take over from Mori Alfeka the position of judge, adviser, and teacher of the Marib Jews in the future. But now he wondered if old Alfeka would continue to teach him after their arrival in Israel. Jews from all over the world were migrating to Israel, and certainly there were among them people who knew much more of religion and the laws than Shalom did. In which case, they would probably choose for themselves a teacher and judge from among these others and reject Shalom. Perhaps he would have to sit in the silversmith shop, acting as a journeyman to his brother, until he rotted. . . . God could just as well have waited a while to let the Jews return to the Holy Land and could have let me first become a teacher in Marib, he thought. Hastily he pushed the thought away, amazed at his daring in not accepting the will of God with gladness and humility.

On the fourth day the journey became even more difficult. The mountains were lower and the paths less steep by this time, but at this lower elevation the heat began to be oppressive again because there were no more cooling breezes. About midday they came to a valley where there were meadows, almost emerald green with the thriving crops. At the edge of the valley was a little village—only a few cube-shaped houses surrounding a well. Accompanied by one of the askari, Mori Alfeka walked to the village to buy food for the travelers and to ask for permission to water their mules at the well. Water is considered a commodity as precious as life itself. Mohammed the Prophet set forth very strict rules for his devout followers, telling them never to deny water to a traveler. The people of the village obeyed the laws, and both the people and the animals were allowed to quench their thirst at the edge of the well. After a good deal of bargaining, the travelers from Marib then bought a little flour, and the women began to prepare the meal over a hastily built fire. All the inhabitants of the village left their houses and came to see the travelers, because they had doubtless never before seen so many men, women, and children at one time.

Both of the askari kept themselves at a distance and fixed their own food. This was the way it had been during the whole trip; even at night, the soldiers had kept out of the way of the others. Their customs and religious laws would not allow them to sit beside a Jew or eat with one. For the most part the Jews and the soldiers didn't speak with each other—at most Mori Alfeka could exchange a few words with them or ask them a question if necessary. Up to this time they had not been helpful in any way except in shooting an occasional mule who had managed to stumble on the stony, steep path and break a leg. But otherwise, if troubles or difficulties arose, such as a pack slipping from a mule's back or a mule becoming contrary and refusing to move, the askari simply looked on almost approvingly. They would not think of pitching in and helping.

After partaking of their hastily prepared midday meal, the travelers proceeded on their way again, and about eventide, they came to a flat mountaintop, which seemed like a good location to spend the night. Soon the women had fires going, and the men unloaded the packs from the mules. The minute the sun disappeared behind the mountains, a chilling wind came up, and the air cooled rapidly. Before long all of them had crawled into their striped blankets and were sound asleep.

Early the following morning Mori Alfeka gathered the men around him for the regular morning prayer. Covering their heads with their blue-bordered prayer shawls, they began in chorus to intone quietly a prayer of thanksgiving for the repose of the previous night. Everyone turned in the direction of the holy city, Jerusalem.

Shalom was not yet thirteen, the age at which, according to the Jewish religion, he would be deemed a man. He did not own a prayer shawl, but he stood beside his brother with his little turban on his head and said the prayers along with the others. Though the grownups stood with their heads bowed, Shalom looked around observantly. Some distance away the women and the small children were preparing to break up camp, and close at hand the mules were searching in the crevices for something edible. Off to the right, about thirty yards from the others, the askari had squatted down on the ground and were talking together, each of them making expansive gestures. Shalom observed that one of the soldiers put his gun behind a boulder, whereupon both of them arose. The unarmed askari slowly approached the group engaged in prayer, while the other loaded his long-barreled shotgun.

Shalom had a feeling they were up to no good. Quickly he ducked behind a tamarisk bush, flattened himself on the ground, and then, sheltered by the cliffs, crept toward the askari who was armed. He had raised his gun. Cautiously Shalom crept along until he was right behind the soldier.

Meanwhile, the other askari had come up to the people who were praying. He drew his wide, curved dagger from his belt, and in a shrill, nervous voice, he cried, "Put your hands up over your heads, you dirty Jews! The person I point to must lay his money pouch at my feet. And anyone who doesn't obey at once will get one of my comrade's bullets in his body. Hurry up now. Out with the money, you heathen dogs!"

The rhythmic prayers came to a rapid halt, and the men, pale and terrified, stared at the shouting askari.

"Well, what are you waiting for? Do you feel the need of having a bullet in your stomach? Up with your hands, I said!" the Yemenite, who by now felt much more sure of himself, shouted. Simultaneously the men raised their arms as the soldier pointed at Mori Alfeka.

"Take the money pouch from around your neck, you old swine, and lay your money here in front of me!"

The face of the elderly leader began to twitch, but there was no way out. One hand had already reached his neck when the other askari let out a loud yell and sank to the

ground. As he fell, he dropped his weapon; it struck against a boulder, and a shot rang out. At the outcry of his comrade and the sound of the shot, the other askari turned instinctively to see what had happened. One of the younger Jews seized this opportunity to run up and hold him from behind.

"Take the dagger away from him!" cried the young man, and two of the other men, who, up to this time, had stood as if turned to stone, ran up and disarmed the flailing, kicking askari. One of them wrenched the dagger out of his hand, and the other undid his cartridge belt. The second askari still lay unconscious on the ground. At this point Shalom's head, and then his whole body, emerged from behind the rock. Cautiously he crept out from his hiding place and grabbed the shotgun that had dropped. Another boy quickly secured the second gun.

It was Shalom who had saved the situation by sneaking up on the Yemenite from behind and hitting him in the head with a large stone. His anger had given him added strength, no doubt, because the askari was still unconscious on the ground.

Mori Alfeka walked over to him and called out to the women, "Bring some water here. He's bleeding!"

Carefully, the old teacher loosened the turban from the soldier's head and, with a wet cloth, began to care for his wound. It wasn't long before the askari regained consciousness and began to moan as he held his head.

5

The Arrival in San'a

The wounded askari and his comrade seemed gloomy and downhearted as they crouched leaning against a rocky cliff. Their hands were tied. Yussef had taken their weapons— the two long-barreled shotguns and their curved daggers. The heads of the Marib Jewish families were holding an advisory council with Mori Alfeka as the leader. They discussed what they were going to do with the two disarmed soldiers. Finally the elderly teacher gave his opinion in the same slow, singing tone of voice he had used when he was called upon to settle a dispute back at the little temple in Marib.

"These two askari—cursed be their names—wanted to rob us of our money. They had in mind afterwards to escape beyond the mountains, to the land of King Ibn Saud, to Saudi Arabia. And here we would have been, stranded without money and without protection. Within a few days, robbers from the mountains might have attacked us and stolen the remainder of our possessions. Thus stripped of everything, we might all have met our destiny here in the mountains. But God, bless His name a thousandfold, did not allow them to complete their evil plans."

Three times Mori Alfeka stroked his thin white beard before continuing.

"If we give them back their weapons, the wretches would be able to make another attempt to catch us off guard. Therefore, are we not all in agreement that they must not have their weapons back?"

The answer came in the form of mumbles of assent and many definitive nods, all of which the old man noted with great satisfaction.

"We'll keep the weapons and let them come along, unarmed, until we get close to San'a. When we can see the large mosque in the city, we can return their guns and daggers to them. Do any of you have any suggestions? I can think of nothing better."

After a short pause, one of the heads-of-family began to speak.

"Mori Alfeka, you have studied the Holy Scriptures all of your life, and if you say that's the right thing, then certainly it's right. But tell me, if these askari must be deprived of their weapons, then who will protect us from the wild bands of robbers in the mountains? And won't they try to run away from us at some point when we're not watching? Then who can lead us? We do not know the paths through these deserted cliffs. And if, with God's help, we ever get to San'a, won't these askari denounce us there? All of us are well aware that possession of a weapon by a Jew is punishable by death and that an even more agonizing death awaits anyone who has forcibly taken a weapon from a soldier."

"Your apprehensions are not completely justified," Mori Alfeka replied. "In the first place, the askari won't try to run away from us because where could they go without their weapons? 'A soldier without his weapon is worth less than a mangy donkey,' says one of our old proverbs. Therefore, they'll stay with us, and they'll show us the way.

"And in the second place"—and at this point the old man joined his thumb and his ring finger, just as if he were counting on his fingers—"we are by no means defenseless and unarmed. Ever since Yussef reached manhood, he has had something to do with weapons in his workshop. He can be our champion and defender."

Yussef was more than a little proud of his important commission, and he nodded eagerly, voicing his consent. Mori Alfeka went on.

"The third and last thing: they won't want to tell anyone that we took their weapons away from them. Neither will they spread the word that we, in spite of the law, put their daggers into our own belts and hung their guns over our own shoulders. Were word to get around about this, the whole city would spit at them, and the Imam would have them beheaded at the market place in San'a. They'll be as silent as the grave, I assure you."

His arguments were convincing, and when Mori Alfeka outlined to the askari the conditions, they agreed with every sign of being relieved about the whole thing. They had been afraid that Mori Alfeka would simply give the order to shoot them, which is usually the case with thieves who are apprehended in Yemen. As a matter of fact, both of the undernourished soldiers experienced a great feeling of relief at not having to carry their heavy weapons and their cartridge belts as they continued the journey.

The way through the mountains led toward the southeast. Both the soldiers went ahead, followed immediately by the proud Yussef with one of the shotguns in his hand. Mori Alfeka, who himself had assumed responsibility for the other gun, was the last one in the caravan. While the advisory council had been in session, Shalom had stood beside his brother. It had been quite forward of him to assume a place among the heads of the families, but no one remarked about it, and he himself felt that he had earned the honor. He had hoped that Mori Alfeka or one of the others would praise him or even reward him for having hit the askari on the head, but no one had said a word about Shalom's performance.

They had been on their way for about half an hour, and Shalom, as before, walked beside his mother, leading the family's mule by a rope. The mule had no great inclination to keep moving, and Shalom had all he could do to convince the stubborn animal, by hitting it with the end of the rope and by using a few uncomplimentary words, that progress was necessary. He had just called the mule an especially uncomplimentary name when a small boy ran up to him.

"Quick, Shalom. Come. Mori Alfeka wants to talk to you."

"Aha," Shalom said to himself. "Now I will receive my well-earned praise." Turning the rope over to his mother, he hurried to his teacher. For a long time Mori Alfeka said nothing, and of course Shalom could not begin a conversation in the presence of his revered and elderly teacher. Finally Mori Alfeka broke the silence.

"You deserve some praise, my son, because you used your eyes to observe and your brain to think. You alone of all of us noticed that the soldiers were plotting some evil deed."

As was the custom, Shalom looked down at the ground and kept silent, but the taste in his mouth was like that of the holidays when Mother served clear melted butter on the pancake-shaped bread. Strictly speaking, the praise was even better than melted butter because it was a rarer gift, and it had come from Mori Alfeka, the wisest among all of the Jews from Marib.

The next words of the old teacher tasted all the more bitter because of the preceding sweetness.

"At the same time you should know, Shalom, that I'm ashamed of you," Mori Alfeka said after a short pause. "I have tried to bring you up to be a pious and well-informed person who would devote his life to an ever deeper searching of the laws and to being an interpreter of the will of God. But instead of being an instrument of peace among the people, you used violence. I had not thought to bring you up as an undisciplined fighter . . ."

At first Shalom felt completely crestfallen because he had expected only praise. Then Mori Alfeka's words began to awaken resentment and rebellion within him.

"I don't understand, venerable Mori Alfeka," he exclaimed heatedly. "Didn't you yourself teach me how Joshua, Gideon, Samson, and our forefathers fought against the Canaanites and other enemies? Every chapter in the Torah speaks of wars and heroes. Isn't that right, Mori Alfeka?"

"Yes and no, both. The persons mentioned in the Holy Scriptures as heroes and army leaders took up arms to defend the Jewish people against aggressors—against those whose purpose was to conquer and imprison the people of Israel, to destroy God's kingdom, and to banish His name from the face of the earth. The Scriptures reserve praise for those who defended a throne. Your name, Shalom, means 'peace.' And you struck one of your fellow men in the head with a stone—so violently that he was badly hurt. That was not worthy of your name."

Shalom became more and more angered by the old man.

He vaguely understood what Mori Alfeka was alluding to, but his whole being protested, and he tried to defend his own rights.

"I don't understand you, beloved teacher. These soldiers wanted to rob us. I wasn't attacking them. I was simply defending *us*. And when you held council with all the heads of the families, you said yourself that if they hadn't been overcome, we might all have perished in these deserted mountains. Didn't I do the right thing when I hit that cursed thief in the head as hard as I could?"

"The soldiers merely wanted to take our money, not our lives. To be sure, I said something about the fact that the incident could have meant the end of all of us, but I said that only to comfort the timid souls. During the two thousand years we Jews have been scattered and separated from the land of Israel, we have never taken up arms, have never defended ourselves with the sword, nor have we ever avenged our enemies. Our weapon is our belief. Our duty in a strange country is to give witness to our belief and to bring peace among people. Don't you see that, my son?"

Reluctantly, Shalom answered as he had long ago learned he must. "I do understand, Mori Alfeka, and I thank you for what you've taught me." Then, without looking back at the elderly man, he returned to his place in the middle of the caravan and took the mule's rope from his mother's hand. Never before, not even for a moment, had it occurred to him that he could doubt anything Mori Alfeka told him or taught him. Often when his brother Yussef or some other adult commanded Shalom to do this or that, he felt a certain stubbornness in himself, although he seldom dared to show it openly. Never once had he felt as if he could stand in opposition to his teacher. But this time he could not accept the fact that Mori Alfeka was right. The more he turned the problem over in his mind, the stronger his conviction grew that he had behaved like a pious, God-fearing Jew when he hit the askari with the stone. "And if anyone tries to rob me or to hurt any of us again, I'll hit *them* in the head, too," he added to himself.

During the three remaining days of the trip to San'a, Shalom did not seek any contact with Mori Alfeka. Neither did he attempt, as he had before, to start a conversation with him at the time of evening prayer. Resentfully, he walked along with the caravan, tugging at the mule's rope, helping silently to unload and load the equipment, but he almost never spoke. He was deeply wounded and defiantly certain he had been right. He felt infinitely alone.

On the morning of the eighth day, a beautiful vista suddenly opened up before the eyes of the travelers. At the foot of the mountains, almost right under them, lay a seemingly endless plain, flat as a pancake. In the blazing morning sun, the plain seemed to have a yellowish, brownish, reddish sheen, and as far as the eye could see there wasn't a single sign of vegetation. There, in the middle of the plain, rose the city of San'a—a city at least two thousand years old— with its cluster of tall buildings, the cupolas of the mosques, and the slender columns of the minarets inside the city wall.

No one ordered them to do so, but everyone stopped still in the middle of the path to stare, with wide-open eyes, at the city that to them appeared so overwhelming. And the city was surely worthy of admiration, even from far more experienced travelers than were the people from Marib. From that height, San'a appeared to be laid out in the form of a figure eight, surrounded by a wall about ten yards high and four or five yards thick.

When they had completed their descent to the plain, both of the soldiers came to Mori Alfeka and begged humbly to be given back their weapons. The old man acceded to their wish. And as soon as they had stuck the daggers in their belts, fastened their cartridge belts across their chests, and taken their guns in hand, these raggedy, thin Yemenites became soldiers again. Mori Alfeka was not content merely to restore their weapons to them. Taking out his money pouch, he gave each of them a silver coin, a rial. The soldiers grinned happily at the shiny coins, and then, bowing eagerly and saluting by lifting their left hands to their turbans, they thanked him for such a generous gift.

Shalom, for his part, viewed the scene with rage and bitterness. If I had had any part in the decision, he thought to himself, they would have had a hard kick as a reward. The scoundrels!

Like victorious army generals, the askari led the procession of the Jews from Marib up to the main gate of San'a. Bab-el-Yemen, which was the name of that particular opening in the city wall, led into the oldest part of the city, and no Jew was allowed to enter through it. Soldiers in dark blue turbans emerged from the barracks just outside the gate. Both of the Marib askari gave an account of the journey to an officer who had a splendid ornamented belt and a huge dagger. Then the officer ordered Mori Alfeka to continue westward alongside the city wall, past two additional gates, and to ask permission to enter the city through the third gate, which was called Bab-el-Ga. This gate led directly to the Jewish quarter, and it was the only one through which the Jews were allowed entry. The officer added that they would have to hurry if they wanted to have a roof over their heads before nightfall because, once darkness came, all the

gates were closed and could be opened only by order of the commandant of the city, the Emir himself. And the Emir would never be bothered to help a handful of Jews from the provinces.

Luck was with the caravan from Marib. They managed to reach the Bab-el-Ga gate before sundown. Upon receiving a quarter rial, one of the askari on guard duty at the gate expressed his willingness to hurry to the leader of the Jews in San'a, the rabbi, and inform him of the arrival of the travelers. A little while later the rabbi himself came to the gate, and the caravan from Marib was allowed to crowd slowly through onto the narrow, winding streets of the Jewish quarter. The first stage of the long journey for Shalom and his friends was at an end.

6

Seeing the City

The Jews in Sanʻa received their fellow Jews from Marib
with hospitality and brotherly feeling. They had been previously advised that they would be coming, and they knew
that the Marib group wanted to go on to Israel. Many
among them were making preparations to follow the example of the Marib Jews, and some of them had already
departed. The Marib Jews were rapidly settled in different
homes, where they were offered food and drink. Shalom
and his family were invited to live in a two-story house right
in the center of the Jewish quarter. The head of the house
was a well-to-do and distinguished man who, even on week-
days, wore a black waistcoat over his striped garment. It
didn't take long for Shalom to discover that Saud ben Levy,
their host, seemed to be some sort of artist. He made designs
for the stucco decorations that the aristocratic Arabs in
Sanʻa used to adorn the facades of their houses.

The long journey through the mountainous terrain had
taken its toll of the wanderers. Their clothing was soiled and
frayed; their feet were blistered; and all of them were thin
and undernourished. It would take them at least a week to
rest, repair their belongings, and care for their weary mules.
Shalom would have liked to move on after a few days'
pause, but this was clearly impossible.

The third day of their stay in San'a was the Sabbath, and the newcomers joined their hosts in going to the temple. There were several temples in the Jewish quarter of San'a, and Shalom and his brother went with Saud ben Levy to the largest of them. From the outside, the temple was not vastly different from the houses. It was gray and completely undecorated. But with its well-balanced proportions and its cushioned seats, it seemed beautiful in comparison to the small one in Marib. The candles that burned in the seven-branched candlesticks at the side of the ark of the covenant were at least three times as large as the ones in Marib, and the scrolls of the Torah here were covered with red velvet, on which the six-pointed star of David was embroidered in shining gold. The temple and the Sabbath services were a tremendous experience for Shalom, but once the holy day was over, the days seemed to drag. He had no desire to read; neither did he want to see his teacher, Mori Alfeka. The heads of the families spent most of their time in the temple, even when there were no services going on, conversing with the elders among the San'a Jews—who by this time had sons and grandsons to take over their work. Shalom couldn't join in all this because it was only for heads of families. Shalom's mother and sister were occupied with preparing food, resting, or washing, and, for that matter, you couldn't enjoy talking with women.

At length Shalom asked his host, the respected Saud, if he would take him into the city so that he could see all the beautiful things he had heard of. Saud promised that he would, but he must have forgotten or been too busy with other things. Half ill with curiosity, Shalom longed to see the tall buildings—often five stories high—the palace of the reigning Imam, the mosques, and all the other unusual and exciting things that a large city has to offer. By this time he had ascertained that the Jews could leave their quarter only if they had a job or errands in other parts of the city. Roaming the city were any number of askari patrols, and if a Jew were caught on the streets without an acceptable excuse, he was locked up. It might take up to two weeks before he could be freed, and there was also the possibility of a heavy fine.

Saud had told Shalom also that the Jewish quarter was set apart from the city by a certain wall, which had only one gate. After evening prayer that gate was closed, and then no Jew could come out from or go into the Jewish quarter. Any Jews caught outside their own quarter could count on severe punishment.

Mounting curiosity gave Shalom no peace, and after five days of waiting in vain for his host to keep his promise, he decided to go into the city on his own the next morning, regardless of the consequences. He had figured out that if an askari were to stop him on the street, he could always say that he had been sent with a message for the stucco artist, Saud ben Levy, from the Jewish quarter.

After morning prayers, Shalom set out. He followed along the wall between the Jewish quarter and the other part of the city until he came to a gate. There he attached himself to a Jew who was walking in the direction of the city, following behind him at a distance of two steps in accordance with oriental custom. The guard thought—and with good reason—that Shalom was the older man's son and let them pass through the gate. To be on the safe side, Shalom tagged behind the stranger another hundred yards or so, and then, when the man turned to the right at a cross street, Shalom turned to the left.

He found himself on a winding but rather wide street, bordered on both sides by thriving, verdant gardens. The boy had lived his whole life in Marib at the edge of the desert and consequently had never before seen so many date palms, fiery red hibiscuses, thorny tamarisk bushes, and other extraordinary trees and plants. Running down the middle of the gardens was a paved canal filled with sparkling crystal-clear water. Previously, Shalom had seen water only in a well, and the canal seemed to him more miraculous than anything else.

In one of the gardens he saw a turbaned man, his legs bare clear up to his knees, with a long-handled wooden spade in hand with which he scooped up water from the canal. In a wide arc, he sprayed the water out over the plants. Shalom guessed that this must be necessary in order for the plants to grow, but deep inside he was disturbed at the thought of these lighthearted city dwellers treating something as precious as water so wastefully.

The sun was quite high in the sky by the time Shalom managed to tear himself away from the mysteries of the gardens, the canals, and the surrounding villas. He began to walk along the streets, which, at that time of day, were rather empty. Soon he came to a square. In the background was a reddish-brown four-story house, decorated with white stucco ornamental designs. Admiringly Shalom stared at the house, which was at least twenty times as large as their little hut in Marib, and came to the conclusion that it must be the Imam's palace. However, as he continued on his way, he caught sight of an even larger and more elegant palace. How big was the Imam's palace, anyway?

He didn't have time to settle the question in his mind because at this point a crowd of men in turbans and women shrouded from top to toe in dark clothing came streaming out of the house. They all hurried along in the same direction. With very little hesitation, Shalom followed them. The road passed by a mosque with shining cupolas, but the people didn't stop there. Instead they continued to walk along the dusty, hard clay path. Shalom was well aware that Jews did not have the right to walk on the foot paths; therefore, he stayed in the middle of the dusty, sandy road. At this point the road began to narrow, and to the right were two palaces even grander than the ones he had seen before. They were embellished with snow-white stucco ornaments all the way from the ground clear up to the flat roof. After a while he came to a city gate.

In the crowd Shalom managed to escape the watchful eyes of the guard. But now his own eyes were truly wide open with astonishment. On the other side of the gate stood four five-story houses, one beside another, and the winding streets were so narrow that the rays of sun could scarcely find their way down between the walls of the houses. Here it was almost like twilight, and the heat was not as oppressive as it was in the open spaces. Granted, the smells were rather offensive in the cool shadows—mutton tallow and heavily seasoned food, to say nothing of the piles of mule dung on the street—for in Yemen the main agent in charge of garbage disposal and street cleaning is the rain. For six or seven months of the year not a drop of rain falls, however, during which time the smells of Yemenite cities can be very unpleasant indeed.

Shalom, accustomed to the fresher air of Marib, soon began to feel nauseated, but perhaps it was also a question of hunger. With all the sights to see, he had lost track of time, and though he did not realize it, it would soon be time for the midday meal. Everywhere in these shadowy streets the city bustled with life. Ragged, barefoot mule drivers passed by with their heavily laden animals, long-legged camels waddled by with their heads high above the pedestrians, and women, shrouded from head to foot in their dark costumes, went in and out of the buildings. On every street corner squatted three or four beggars asking loudly for alms. Most of the beggars were blind, due to trachoma, a widespread eye disease in Yemen, and a few of them were missing a hand or an arm, a sign that at one point they had been caught stealing and, as punishment, had been disfigured. Shalom also noticed that in this part of the city some of the men had much wider belts, turbans of two or three different brilliant colors, and walked around carrying much larger and more magnificent daggers than others he had seen. Aristocrats such as these were always accompanied by a couple of armed servants walking at the side of their masters, crying at the tops of their lungs, "Make way. Make way for our master, the respected Ibn Salem of the shining presence." Of course, the names differed. These "respected" and "shining" persons stood out from the ordinary mortals because they wore a sort of blue-black coloring on their eyelids and under their eyes. The wealthier citizens of Yemen colored the skin around their eyes with antimony as a protection against infectious eye diseases.

Soon Shalom found himself right in the center of a pushing, slowly moving throng of people. His wanderings had brought him to the business district of San'a—to the bazaar. On both sides of its streets were low, barracks-like buildings, which opened out onto the street. The small, narrow stalls were filled to the brim with the wares of the merchants who themselves crouched outside on the streets, advertis-

ing their stocks in shrill Arabian voices. On one of these streets, bearded merchants sold carpets with striped or geometric patterns; the next street was the domain of the sandal makers; the third belonged to coppersmiths, who hammered out coffee cups, kettles, and other utensils. And on the street of the silversmiths, anyone could stand and admire the craftsmanship of the owners right from the street. Within the confines of the bazaar the Yemenites could find any product they needed. But of course their needs were comparatively few.

It didn't take Shalom long to find out that there were quite a few Jews among the craftsmen in the bazaar. They were especially in evidence among the jewelers and the dealers in fine clothing. One of the latter, an emaciated old man, beckoned to Shalom.

"What are you doing here in the bazaar, Jew boy?"

Shalom had no desire to lie to this old man who had addressed him in such a mild and friendly way, so he said that he was out taking a look at the city.

"You're one of the Jews from Marib, aren't you? You've done wrong in daring to come into this part of the city alone, my son. You are exposing yourself to danger, and you know the saying: 'Foolish is he who exposes himself to danger.' Can you tell me where that passage is to be found in the Holy Scriptures?"

"Yes, it's in the Book of Proverbs."

"Absolutely right. You don't seem to be so stupid in spite of the fact that you have put yourself unnecessarily in the way of danger. Have you had anything to eat today?"

The old man took out a hand-loomed lunchbag. Out of it came two loaves of bread, somewhat bigger than the palm of your hand, which were wrapped in clean white linen. There were also a silver canteen containing an oily sauce and a clay crock containing fresh water.

With some water from the crock, the old man washed his hands, after which he motioned to Shalom to follow his example. Then both of them turned eastward, in the direction in which the holy city of Jerusalem was located, far, far away, and recited their lunch-time prayer. After that the old man blessed the food. Dipping the bread in the sauce, both of them began to eat.

"Thank you, brother of my father, for giving me food and drink and for sharing your meal with me. May the Lord reward you and bless your name and that of your kin," said Shalom in accordance with the traditional form of thanksgiving, just as soon as the small meal had been consumed.

"Very well said, my son," the old man replied. "May the nourishment be to your benefit, and may our God strengthen you. Now stay here with me, and we'll go back to the Jewish quarter together before time for evening prayers."

Shalom thanked the old man for his thoughtfulness and sat down beside him just outside the stall. Now and then a customer came along and felt the quality of his linens and silks.

Soon the streets of the bazaar were almost deserted, with only a few remaining customers here and there. A muezzin, the crier at the mosque, announced in a piercing voice from the balcony of a nearby minaret, "The time has come for the midday prayers. Say your prayers, you who are faithful. There is no God but Allah, and Mohammed is His Prophet."

The time of day had come for all work to cease. The faithful said their prayers, ate their food, and went off to rest. The well-to-do and the aristocrats did so in the coolest room in the top story of their houses; the poor crept away somewhere to rest in the shade of a wall.

Even the old man moved into the farthest corner of his shop, put his head down on a small cushion, and pointed out a place for Shalom to take a nap. And a few minutes later, both of them were sleeping.

7

Aden, the Second Stop

Shalom got home quite late. After accompanying the old clothing dealer through the gate, he avoided going directly home, since he was afraid of the reception awaiting him there. He had been gone all day, and by this time Yussef would surely be aware of the fact that he had been out in the Arabian city.

The beating his brother gave him later exceeded even his wildest apprehensions. Yussef was beside himself with rage. Calling Shalom every abominable and unpleasant name he could think of, he made good use of his fists, the palms of his hands, and his feet. Yussef was the youngest of the heads-of-family in Marib, and for this reason he was doubly ashamed that it was a member of his family who had been guilty of such a dreadful lapse.

His mother's pleas and tears were no match for Yussef's rage, and he might well have beaten Shalom half to death if Mori Alfeka hadn't put in an appearance. The old teacher told Yussef to cease the blows, but he was unable to halt the stream of abusive words. Finally, Mori Alfeka was forced to throw him out of the kitchen.

As soon as teacher and pupil were alone, Mori Alfeka began to speak in a low but serious voice. He reminded Shalom of his duty to be obedient and humble, sprinkling

71

his lecture with many quotations from the Holy Scriptures. The old man suspected that Shalom's headstrong expedition into the city was simply a part of the general feeling of rebellion that had been plaguing the boy ever since the attempted robbery up in the mountains.

With his head bowed, Shalom took his medicine. Deep down inside he admitted that he had behaved badly, but he felt, too, that the others had treated him with unjustifiable strictness. Why hadn't Saud ben Levy kept his promise and showed him the city? Shalom had no chance to explain that sheer inquisitiveness had caused him to embark upon his adventure. Not even if Mori Alfeka had asked him outright could he have put into words the thoughts that were presently tumbling about in his head.

For another three days the Marib Jews enjoyed the hospitality of their fellow Jews, but early on Monday morning, they loaded their few possessions onto the mules, and the little caravan assembled at the gate leading out from the Jewish quarter. Here, expressing their final gratitude, they parted. Singing one of the psalms of David, they began to make their way across the deserted flatlands. Three families from San'a had joined them. The heads of two of these families had several times previously traveled southward to Aden, and they knew the terrain. They now led the procession of wanderers.

The way between San'a and Aden, the largest port city in the Arabian peninsula, has been much traveled by caravans for over three thousand years. At one time it was regarded as one of the most important routes of commerce in the world. But that was a long, long time ago, and the ancient road nowadays is not in such good condition, nor is it so usable, as it was in the Middle Ages.

Even before the morning had passed, they were approaching the southern edge of the San'a plain and were close to the rocky terrain of the high mountains. From there the path grew steeper and steeper. Mountains, some of them nine thousand feet high, rose to the sides of the narrow, stony path. At noon they rested high above sea level. At that elevation the temperature was comfortable, which eased the journey, but the older people had a hard time breathing in the rarefied air. Some of them even got nosebleeds.

In the afternoon of the second day they were quite near the city of Dhamar. And there for a day they rested, building up their strength for the steep climbs that were to come.

In spite of the high mountains, this particular part of Yemen was thickly populated. In the valleys there were nicely cultivated fields in which could be grown tobacco, corn, and coffee.

Shortly after their departure from Dhamar, they met a large caravan. Twenty camels, heavily laden with sacks, progressed one after the other along the narrow path, carrying salt to San'a from a nearby mine. The road sloped down toward a narrow valley, divided in the middle by a river bed. They spent the night in a small village in the lowlands and also bought a good many provisions. And it was a good thing they did. The following evening they approached the city of Rathma, and this city, which normally had a population of about three thousand, was full to overflowing with Jews.

Like the people from Marib, these Jews were on the way to Aden, and from there they wanted to continue on to Israel. They had come from every corner of Yemen but had been obliged to stay in Rathma. There they had been met by the news that the Sultan of Lahei, the ruler of one of the

tribes in the territory of Aden, refused to let the Jews go across his land without paying three rials per person. There were not many who could afford to pay the Sultan's price, and consequently, four messengers had been sent down to Aden to seek help from fellow Jews there. However, no reply had as yet been forthcoming.

The crowded conditions pushed up the prices of groceries and made the business of finding shelter for the night in the city well nigh impossible. The Jews from Marib had to sleep out in the open—insofar as this was possible. Persistent flies and other insects swarmed around everywhere. Mori Alfeka and the heads of the families had agreed that they must con-

tinue their trip early in the morning. They had taken stock of their resources and decided that they could afford to pay the price the Sultan was demanding.

The following three days were the worst of the whole trip. The road was very hilly, and two of the mules fell, each breaking a leg, and had to be put to death. Jews, as well as Arabs, are forbidden by their religion to eat the meat of either mules or horses, and the ground was so stony that it was completely impossible to bury the bodies of the animals. Therefore, they had to content themselves with placing several stones on them and leaving them there as prey for eagles and vultures. The caravan had gone scarcely more than a

few hundred yards from the site before the black birds began to circle high above the animals' dead bodies.

Following the Mosaic law, the Marib Jews spent Saturday
at rest. The hardships of the trip had made them all so thin
and so fatigued that they merely lay there apathetically the
whole day, lacking the strength to talk to one another. The
men said the prayers of the Sabbath in low, mumbling
voices.

At the close of the Sabbath, in the evening, the women
had recovered sufficiently to build a fire and make porridge
out of the ground meal that was left. They were just about
to partake of this scanty repast when a small group of people
with one mule approached their camp site. They too were
Jews, and had already made an attempt to cross the territory of the Sultan of Lahei. The Sultan had taken their payments and afterwards had chased them back across the
border.

When the Marib women heard that, they began to weep
and wail, and even the children began to cry, although they
had no idea of what it was all about. Crestfallen, the men sat
motionless, staring straight ahead. Mori Alfcka, who up to
this point had always been able to comfort and cheer up the
people in the caravan, sat and stroked his white beard, never
saying a word. One of the newcomers, his voice breaking,
said that he had made up his mind to return to his village
in Yemen. "Obviously it isn't God's will to allow us to get to
Israel!" he said in exhaustion. The moment Mori Alfeka
heard that his strength increased.

"Turn around and go back? Never! If there is a David
reigning in Jerusalem and if Israel has risen again from its
ashes, it is then our duty to go there. For forty years Moses
roamed around in the desert with his people. And still the

Jews didn't have to return to bondage. We must not fail in our duty. God—the God of Abraham, Isaac, and Jacob—will help us!"

He then turned to the men from San'a who had thus far been their guides.

"Do you know of any other way to get to Aden than the one that crosses the territory of the thrice confounded Sultan of Lahei?"

Putting their heads together, the three men from San'a, after a short consultation, said that, if the caravan were to head toward Bitha, they would come to the land of the Sultan of Kuri. They said, to be sure, that none of them had ever been there themselves, but that it was not unthinkable that the ruler of the Bedouins of Kuri might prove to be more humane than the Sultan of Lahei. They added that Bitha was about two days' journey eastward from the place where they were then encamped.

In a voice that did not invite any opposition, Mori Alfeka explained that the next morning they would head for Bitha instead of following the way they had originally planned. At dawn they broke camp, and the newcomers joined the group from Marib. It took them three days to make the two days' journey. Everyone was dead tired. Many of them had sores on their legs or hands as a result of the insect bites, and the hot sand felt like fire beneath the soles of their feet.

On the afternoon of the third day they saw, at the horizon, something resembling a cloud of dust. It seemed to be coming closer very rapidly. Gradually they realized that the cloud of dust was being stirred up by a group of galloping riders. As the riders reached the caravan, they hastily surrounded the tired, ragged people. One of the riders, a

bearded man, dismounted and, in a commanding tone of
voice, began to speak.

"I wish to talk with the leader of the caravan. Come here
in front of me and tell me who you are and where you are
going."

Mori Alfeka trudged up and greeted the Bedouin, bowing
deeply three times. In a respectful tone of voice and in
Arabic, he said that they were Jews from Yemen and that
they were on the way to the city of Aden. He described the
route they had in mind and gave the names of all the heads
of the families.

The bearded commander turned out to be the ruler of the
Bedouins of Kuri. As he listened to Alfeka's story, he flew
into a towering rage and cursed the Jews who, without permission, had dared to set their shabby feet on his ground.
He threatened to chase all of them straight back to Yemen.

Mori Alfeka was not greatly impressed by the salty swear-
ing and cursing. Quietly and unassumingly, he replied.

"Most honored Sultan, ruler and governor of the tribe of
Kuri, may the eternal God bless you and your kin. Permit
your unworthy servant to remind you of one of the laws of
the great prophet Mohammed: 'Help the destitute, although
they number themselves not among the faithful. Do not turn
away the hungry who ask of you food and drink, neither
deny the traveler your hospitality.' Thus it is written in the
Koran. I'm sure that you, most laudable Sultan and ruler,
would scarcely wish to go against the laws of the Koran. We
are travelers who, trusting in your good heartedness, desire
to cross your territory. And we have suffered many things.
Just look at our children—thirsty and starving!"

The ruler of the Bedouins was clearly amazed at this
ragged Jew who could recite portions of the Koran and who

did not fear him, in spite of the fact that he had at his command over three hundred armed, mounted Bedouins. In a somewhat milder tone of voice he began to deal with Mori Alfeka and, with the innate suspiciousness of the Arab, questioned him as to all the details of their journey. Finally he gave Alfeka his decision.

"All of you are filthy, heathenish curs. But the laws of the Koran were laid down to protect even such as you, so enormous was the grace of our great prophet Mohammed. With the payment of two rials per family, you may continue on your way in peace!"

By bowing deeply three times, Mori Alfeka showed his gratitude and, with outstretched arms, bestowed his blessing on the Sultan. The riders in the blue burnooses remained with the caravan, and they headed across the desert toward a palm-encircled spring, which served as the dwelling place of the Kuri tribe. They were permitted to water their animals and to quench their own thirst. In addition, they were able to buy flour and oil and two sheep. The sheep were slaughtered, after which the women prepared the evening meal over a fire, the fuel for which was hastily gathered horse and camel dung.

The next morning the Sultan requested the Jews to continue their journey forthwith, but when he observed the pathetic condition of most of the members of the caravan, he took back his request. Upon the payment of still another rial per family, he let them spend an additional day at the spring. For three days they remained with the Kuri Bedouins, paying the required fee each day. But on the fourth day, they could not afford to stay any longer. The money pouches the men wore around their necks were completely empty. A good many of the Jews lay sick with fever. Even Shalom had been a victim of it, and he lay half conscious between his mother and sister. Now and then Yussef fetched water for them from the spring.

The Sultan of Kuri realized that they couldn't continue their journey. Therefore, he sent a couple of riders to the British governor in Aden. The next morning, two trucks arrived at the spring in the desert to take the ill, exhausted Jews to the hospital in El Hasched. This settlement, located in a barren district near Aden, was expecting several thousand Yemenite Jews on their way to Israel, to the Holy Land.

Carefully, the chauffeurs from the hospital placed the sick in the trucks; those who were well enough carried their own bundles and possessions. There was not much to carry because in the course of the long journey almost everything they owned had worn out or been broken. The only unscathed objects were the three parchment scrolls of the Torah from the temple in Marib. These they guarded almost with their lives. The last one to climb up onto the truck was Mori Alfeka. He left the mules with the Sultan of Kuri as a thank offering for all his help.

Shalom knew nothing of all this. He simply lay there, unconscious, racked with fever. For the first time in his life he could have seen an automobile—a vehicle that moved without horse power—but opportunity passed him by.

Apathetically the Marib emigrants sat on the trucks watching over their sick. The drivers started the motors, waved good-by to the assembled Bedouins, and took off. The wanderers had at last completed the final stage of the journey to the settlement of El Hasched.

8

In Expectation of the Miracle

At the hospital Shalom soon got better. Rest and nourishing food made a great difference, and after a couple of days he could leave his sick bed. From the storeroom, the nurse Ingrid got him a pair of shorts, a striped, short-sleeved jersey, and a pair of tennis shoes. On his head he proudly wore a linen cap with an eyeshade, which had no doubt belonged to an American boy at one time.

Shalom was immeasurably puffed up over his new clothing, the like of which he had never seen in Yemen. At first he squatted down beside the bed of one patient and then another, indulging in long conversations with them. But he soon wearied of these conversations. Each had exactly the same things to tell—that they had heard there was a new Jewish state, that they had come to find it, and that they had had to endure much suffering. Having heard enough of these stories, Shalom begged Ingrid to give him something to do. The blond nurse had a good many patients to care for, and she gratefully accepted his offer. But, alas, he wasn't much help because the minute he found out what was expected of him, he refused stubbornly and absolutely. Among the nurse's duties was to serve food to the patients and to wash their dishes later on. And her responsibilities included the cleaning both of the small wards and the making of the pa-

tients' beds as well. In some of the other more permanent
hospitals, this sort of work was assigned to helpers or cleaning personnel, but the hospital at El Hasched was an improvised one, and there was a chronic shortage of help.

With great energy, Ingrid tried to teach Shalom how to
handle a broom, dustpan, duster, and such like. But no
matter how much the young Jewish boy admired her, he
refused to have anything to do with these objects. And she
couldn't under any circumstances talk him into helping her
with the dishes. As soon as there was any talk of cleaning or
doing dishes, he simply shook his head and sorrowfully
turned his back.

At first Ingrid couldn't understand the boy's arbitrary re-
fusals, and one evening as they sat at ease, each with a glass
of milk in hand, she asked him outright for an explanation.
He was reluctant to answer, and not until Ingrid finally
threatened to break up their friendship, with its precious
talks in the evening, did he explain at last.

"You're trying to make me do women's work. If ever a
Yemenite saw me doing work like that, he'd immediately tell
all the others, and my reputation would be ruined forever.
Never again would a man from Yemen regard me as a man,
and what's more, even the women would laugh at me."

In vain Ingrid tried to explain to him that men in Israel
didn't feel there was so much difference in "masculine" and
"feminine" jobs and that a good many men were employed
in "feminine" jobs, and vice versa. He seemed to be paying
no attention when she told him that women even served in
the Israeli Army. In the Middle East, men for thousands of
years have thought of women as a lower order of the species,
always subordinate to men. Shalom had grown up with this
outlook, had seen it practiced in his environment, and de-

spite Ingrid's great influence over him, he couldn't be moved from his position.

As a result, Shalom was bored at the hospital. Most of his time was spent in dreaming of Israel. These were happy dreams in full color—of a country with date palms and hibiscus plants, lots of shade, beautiful marble basins with cool, clear water. He recalled the lovely gardens in San'a and decided that the whole country of Israel must be like that. And the houses? Well, surely they were still higher than the ones he had seen in the capital city of Yemen, the façades were of course more beautifully ornamented, and the interiors of all the houses were just as cool and as elegant as was the finest palace in the whole of San'a. And naturally every single house in Israel had a gigantic white refrigerator out of which golden-haired women, all resembling Ingrid, would take ice-cold milk for the men.

In spite of these pleasant reveries, he was quite delighted when the doctor with the glasses, who was making his rounds one day, told him that he was well and that he could leave the hospital the next morning. "New travelers have arrived, and we have to make room for their sick," Ingrid said by way of explanation.

Outside in the settlement, he soon found his family and his friends from Marib. With a cry of joy his mother greeted him, but his brother Yussef didn't seem especially delighted to see him again. He had not forgotten that the boy had disgraced himself and his family with his sight-seeing expedition in San'a. The elderly schoolteacher, Mori Alfeka, greeted him amiably and asked how things had been in the hospital, but when Shalom told him about Ingrid, the doctor with the glasses, and all the technical wonders, he shook his head thoughtfully.

The refugees in the El Hasched settlement found themselves in the midst of a situation that gave them a fine opportunity to practice their oriental patience and that they accepted without protest. The passage of time disturbed them very little. They were convinced that, since the miracle had happened to make Israel rise again after two thousand years, another miracle would surely happen so that the Jews would be able to make their way to the Holy Land of their forefathers.

But Shalom was not able to share in their tranquillity. All the new things he was seeing tumbled about constantly in his thoughts. In order to counteract his restlessness, he went on long expeditions through the tent-lined streets of the settlement. Usually he had as his destination the barracks or the windows of the management quarters and the hospital. In great curiosity he stared through the windowpanes, observing people who were either typewriting or talking on the telephone.

Sometimes he was chased away, but quite often no one paid the slightest attention to him. They simply let him stand there and stare. On one of his expeditions he came to a little open area behind the barracks, where a truck and three jeeps were parked. All the inhabitants of the settlement were familiar with these vehicles because they were often seen on the main road between the barracks and the main entrance gate, engulfed in a sea of thick dust. The Yemenites referred to the automobiles as "miracle chariots," since, according to the rabbi, they were propelled by the will of God. Shalom felt that the explanation was eminently sensible. If a vehicle could move without horses, certainly a miracle of some sort was involved.

But now that he was standing so close to the cars, he decided to take a little closer look at them. On the ground beside the truck was a tarpaulin on which variously shaped pieces of metal had been carelessly tossed. Crouching down on his hands and knees in order to inspect these strange metal objects, he reached for one of them.

"Get your paws away from there, you!" an angry voice cried just a split second later.

In astonishment Shalom looked around, but he couldn't see anyone. In terror he remembered how a mysterious voice had called to Moses from the burning bush. In his fright he bowed his head to the ground and covered his face with his hands, scarcely daring to think what might happen next.

"What in the world is the matter with you, boy? Why are you trying to hide yourself in the sand? I'm certainly not a cannibal."

The voice seemed to come from the immediate vicinity. As Shalom cautiously lifted his eyes, he saw a red-haired man with grease all over his face. His clothes were covered with black spots, and his oily, dirty hands glistened in the strong sunlight.

"I'm lost," Shalom said to himself. "This is the end of me. This must be the Devil himself," he decided, and the fact that the huge-fisted, oil-covered man had crept out from under the miracle chariot served to confirm his conclusion.

"Don't sit there blinking like a scared rabbit. Up with you. Go on home to your father. Just get out of here."

"I haven't got a father," Shalom stammered. "And please don't hurt me. I only wanted to get a good look at the miracle chariot."

The red-haired man grinned, took an oily rag from his overalls pocket, wiped his fingers, and at length lit a cigarette. Then he sat down crosslegged on the running board

of the truck and, in a somewhat more friendly tone of voice, said, "Run along, fellow. This old heap of junk is nothing to look at."

"I want to see how the chariot is propelled by the will of God instead of by horses."

"The darned thing *doesn't* run by the will of God, and that's its main trouble at the moment. That's the reason I'm poking around underneath the truck, and in this insufferable heat, too. Come here, you scamp, and I'll show you how the motor runs. This will be of more use to you in Israel than if you know the whole Bible from memory."

The red-haired driver was an Israeli, born and brought up in that country, and therefore he was a so-called "sabra," which is actually a name for a member of the cactus family. It is said that those born in Israel resemble the fruit of this plant—thorny on the outside but nice and pleasant under the shell. In the space of fifteen minutes he showed Shalom all there was to see of the motor, explaining how it worked and asking every once in a while, "Do you understand, you little scamp?" The boy simply nodded because he couldn't comprehend even half of these words, which he had never before heard in his life. "Carburetor," "accumulator," "gas pedal," and the like neither appeared in the Bible nor were they in the Marib Jewish vocabulary.

"Well, at least you understand that this pile of junk is far from a miracle. But now you'd better hurry home because it will soon be time for supper, and there probably won't be any melted butter left for you if you get home too late."

"But may I come here again tomorrow, Chaver . . ."

"My name is Yitzhak. What's yours?"

"Shalom. And can I come back?"

"Come along if you don't have anything else to do. But

I'm not too sure that I'll be here because a lot of times I have to drive. In that case, I'll be here the next day. But hurry along now . . ."

"Chaver Yitzhak," Shalom repeated to himself that evening before he fell asleep. "Chaver" is the Hebrew word for "brother," and the term is used only when one Jew addresses another. But could these people really be Jews— Yitzhak, golden-haired Ingrid from the hospital, and the doctor? Apparently so, because they were from Israel. But perhaps there were all sorts of people there—not just Jews. To be sure, they spoke Hebrew, even if it wasn't in quite the same dialect as the Yemenites. But it wasn't necessary for one to be a Jew to learn Hebrew. One thing was certain. None of them looked like a Jew. Neither man had a beard; neither had a long curl growing from his temples as every Jew should. "I'll just have to ask Yitzhak tomorrow," Shalom decided finally.

He was in luck. The driver was there the next morning. The repair job was finished, and for the moment he had no driving assignment, so he was sitting in the shade reading an Israeli newspaper in peace and quiet. Shalom squatted down in front of him and waited politely for Yitzhak, the elder of the two, to begin the conversation. This was the custom of the Yemenites.

"Now, Shalom. You haven't forgotten what a driving shaft is for, have you?" Yitzhak eventually asked. Once again they went over to see the motor, and once again he named all the parts and told how they worked. He finished by starting up the motor and driving once around the parking lot. Excited and attentive, Shalom sat beside him in the truck and studied his every movement. Eventually the driver grew tired of the lesson and sat down again in the shade.

Shalom felt that the time was ripe to ask the question he had thought so much about the previous evening.

"Am I a Jew? Ask me questions like that any time because those are the kinds I can answer. Dumb questions. Who do you take me for, anyway—the Pope or the King of Siam? I hope to tell you I'm a Jew. I was once a sergeant in the Israeli Army, and I fought against the Arab legions at the Jerusalem front. My father was a cantor somewhere in Hungary before he emigrated to Israel. My old man had a beard that reached clear down to his knees. Am I a Jew!"

"But then why don't you have a beard and why no curl growing at your temples? And why don't you believe that God is capable of performing miracles?"

Yitzhak was a simple man whose interest in books was not overwhelming, but still he had his own way of looking at things. He proceeded to explain to Shalom that the religious laws of Judaism were certainly appropriate to the times when they had been established two or three thousand years ago, when people lived entirely differently from the way they do nowadays. "But there has been much progress in the world since that time, and most of the old scriptural laws have hindered, not helped, development. Don't you see, Shalom, that if we spent all our time saying our prayers and concentrating on keeping to the letter of the law, we'd never have time left over for building up the country. All the bearded rabbis put together could never have driven out the Arabs, and they couldn't have built modern apartment houses, roads, or irrigation canals for the agricultural areas, either."

These words seemed like heresy to Shalom's ears, mostly because he had no knowledge of the superhuman efforts the colonists had put forth in order to make their neglected, barren country into a habitable, fertile place. He had never been given the opportunity of learning much other than that God would protect him in every circumstance if only he committed great portions of the Scriptures to memory and lived according to the holy laws. His whole world seemed to collapse in front of his eyes as he heard the red-haired driver talking in this fashion.

"Well, if 'miracle chariots' aren't miracles and if miracles never happen, then tell me how are we ever going to get to Israel from here? Our rabbi tells us that we are going to fly there on eagles' wings . . ."

"Look here. You know sometimes your old bearded guys stretch the truth a little. My own old man was just like that himself. There wasn't a technical advance that could surprise him. Naturally, he didn't understand one of them, but no matter how I tried to explain them to him, he just kept repeating, calmly but firmly, that the sound coming over a radio set was caused by the fact that God set the air waves in motion."

"Well, then, it's true that eagles are coming to get us?" asked Shalom with a gleam of hope in his eyes. "And that we're going to get to Israel after all?"

"You're going to get to Israel, all right. That one thing is sure. But you'll have to make do with an airplane instead of eagles' wings. But airplanes have wings, too."

Then the red-haired driver proceeded to tell the eagerly attentive Shalom that the road from Aden—or, rather, from the settlement in El Hasched—passed straight through the Arabian desert, that is, the road, such as it was. But even with the best Land-Rovers or jeeps, the journey would take, at a conservative estimate, several weeks. "The desert is all inside Saudi Arabian territory," he explained, "and since the

ruler of that territory is dead set against the existence of a
Jewish state and wants to do away with it entirely, he and a
bunch of other Arabian leaders have declared war on Israel.
Of course, the Israeli Army managed to drive back their
superior forces and put them to flight, but all this hasn't
made the ruler of Saudi Arabia any friendlier. On the contrary."

Thus it was out of the question that the Yemenite Jews
from the El Hasched settlement would be allowed to cross
the Saudi Arabian territory. In order to get them to Israel,
several American Jewish refugee committees had banded
together and chartered a huge plane, which was going to be
used to transport the refugees across the Red Sea into Israel,
since the air space was not under the jurisdiction of the Arab
countries. Yitzhak gave a short summary of why and how
an airplane could fly.

"I understand," Shalom said. "But now tell me when we
can expect the plane."

"Just a matter of a few days. We got a radio message
from Israel saying that the plane had arrived there and that
it would soon make a trip here to get its first load of passengers. It's lucky that you Yemenites are so small and thin
because they'll be able to stuff in something like a hundred
and twenty-five or a hundred and fifty of you at one time in
the air shuttle. But you mustn't say a word about all this to
anyone, Shalom. It's enough that you know; you don't need
to say anything at all that would disturb the others. And all
the stuff we talked about in connection with religion you
should just keep to yourself. Far be it from me to talk anyone out of his beliefs, because I think everyone has to
work out his own salvation. If your friends like going around

with beards in this infernal heat, I say let them grow beards
so long that they'll stumble over them!"

Shalom promised not to say anything, and he was true
to his word. The thought that he knew something more than
even Mori Alfeka or the honorable rabbi in San'a filled him
with great pride. The next afternoon after their prayers,
when the Marib men sat in the shade of a tent talking about
the miracles that had already happened to them and those
that were surely to come, Shalom was forced to laugh up
his sleeve at all of them. He was neither educated nor ma-
ture enough to be able to understand how wonderful and
worthwhile the movingly naive beliefs of the others really
were. Neither could he perceive that these deep beliefs—
which the Jews, even after two thousand years of homeless-
ness, had not given up in their alien environment—were
unique. The Jews and their culture had not been obliterated
as had so many of the other ancient cultures.

One scorchingly hot morning, two days later, a glistening
silver airplane appeared over the El Hasched settlement.
Flying low, it circled the tent city twice, while its propellers
made the air hum with their noise.

This sound, so unusual, caused the people to rush out of
their tents, turn their faces upward, and stare at the circling
plane.

A shrill voice shouted, "The Lord God has sent us a
silver bird."

And as if on command, four thousand Yemenite Jews—
men, women and children—bowed down to the ground and,
with their arms lifted up, recited the creed of their faith:

"Hear, O Israel! The Lord our God; the Lord is one."

9

On Eagles' Wings

The exodus of the Yemenite Jews from one of the most backward countries in the world, their temporary quarters in the El Hasched settlement, and their burning longing to return to the land of their forefathers had, with the help of the radio and the press, been made known all over the Western world. The American Jewish refugee committee had chartered several planes to transport the refugees to Israel. The first of these, a DC-4 Douglas Skymaster, landed on the fifteenth of December, 1948, at the airport in Aden, when the first group of Yemenite Jews from El Hasched went aboard.

Approximately four weeks later it was Shalom and his friends' turn. The officials of the settlement tried, insofar as was possible, to see that people from the same village or city were together in the same plane. The Marib Jews were able to go aboard the Skymaster in a group. Very early in "Operation Flying Carpet," the upholstered seats and the small kitchenette had been removed from the plane so as to make room for as many passengers as possible. On each side of the cabin, they had installed simple benches, leaving only a small aisle free in the middle. In this way they were able to pack in a hundred people at one time. An Israeli girl served as the stewardess on the plane.

The Yemenites behaved calmly and with their usual oriental dignity. The only sign of emotion displayed over what to them was an utterly extraordinary experience was that the men covered their heads with their shawls and prayed aloud during the entire trip. Shalom spent every minute looking out of the round window of the plane with enormous interest. When it was flying low, he could see the Red Sea below and, to the right and the left respectively, the reddish-gold coastal lines of Arabia and Africa.

When they were about three hours out of Aden, the little children began to complain that they were hungry. Actually, it was just about the time of day that they had been accustomed to receiving their daily food rations in the settlement.

The mothers, who were dressed in their very best and festooned with all sorts of silver ornaments, tried in vain to calm their youngsters, but not even a nasty look from the head of the family helped. At length, the women decided to take matters into their own hands.

At that point the stewardess was sitting in the pilot's cabin with a clipboard on her lap, writing the report she had to hand in to the airport officials at Lod. But suddenly the captain of the plane, Mr. McGuire, stuck his nose into the air.

"Harry! Leah!" he said to the others. "Don't you smell smoke?"

"By golly, you're right," the copilot agreed. Quickly he glanced at the instrument board and found, to his vast relief, that everything was functioning just as it should. Moreover, the noise of the motor was even and quiet. Nothing seemed to be wrong.

A sudden hunch made Leah jump up from her seat. As

she opened the door leading to the passenger cabin, smoke began to pour through. Immediately the stewardess and the copilot rushed out to see where it was coming from. In the aisle between the seats, they discovered a small burning pile of newspapers and little pieces of wood, beside which one of the women squatted. She was holding a little kettle of food over the fire.

The copilot did a wild war dance with his number thirteen shoes and managed to stamp out the fire quickly and effectively. The woman with the kettle began to scream wildly and tried with all her might to shove aside this gangly American who was putting out her fire.

"Idiotic woman! You'll set the whole plane on fire. I've seen some stupid things in my life, but never anything to equal this. Building a fire in the middle of an airplane! Do you think we're still sitting in the middle of the desert?" shouted the copilot, whose face was flaming with exertion and annoyance. In a flash Leah had things under control. First she poured a mug of water on the dying embers; then she explained to the woman that it was highly unusual, as well as perilous, to build a fire in an airplane. Finally she managed to push the angry copilot back into his own cabin again.

The whole episode was over in a few minutes, after which the passengers on the plane simply sat calmly, jammed closely together. But the smell of smoke lingered in the air, which was already heavy with human perspiration.

Soon the youngsters began again to cry for food, but this time Leah had taken the proper measures. Immediately she began to pass sandwiches, hard-boiled eggs, and tea to the passengers. The children were each given a glass of milk.

Having eaten, Shalom made his way up to the door be-

tween the passenger cabin and the cockpit. Every time anyone opened the door, he stared longingly at both of the
pilots, the strange steering mechanisms, and all the different
buttons surrounding the pilot's seat. He would have given
anything in the world to go in with these two Americans
and get a closer look at how they managed to fly the plane.
Yitzhak the driver had of course told him how you piloted
a plane, and he knew about the workings of the motor, too.
But still he didn't have the nerve to ask the stewardess if he
could go in where the pilots were.

His eyes grew tired from staring out of the little round
window, and the smoky, heavy air didn't help any. Also,
his body ached from the strange way of sitting on benches.

So, after a while, he gave up and sat on the floor on his
haunches instead, as most of the other passengers had already done. His stomach was a little unsettled, thanks to the
movements of the plane. Closing his eyes, he began to go
over in his mind the many events of the last few months. In
El Hasched he had not paid much attention to Mori Alfeka,
the man whom he had admired so much in Marib. A little
shamefully he admitted to himself that his attachment to and
admiration for the elderly man wasn't so great any longer.
And to think that at one time back home he had dreamed
of the day when he would be the teacher and would in-
terpret the laws for his congregation. The redheaded Yitzhak
had told him there was a great supply of rabbis in Israel

but that the new Jewish state had a much greater need for working people who were good at their craft than for those who had simply buried themselves in the Scriptures. Now Shalom began to dream of quite a different future. As he sat there, his fantasy turned to the day when he would be a pilot whose plane would go after Jews the world over and bring them to Israel.

At the airport in Aden he had watched the two American fliers closely as they checked things on the plane, all this before he went aboard the Skymaster. One of them sat in the pilot's seat, pushing different buttons and switches, while the other one examined the propellers, waved signals at various people, and even climbed up onto the wings. What an unforgettable sensation it had been when the plane, after a long ride down the runway, had finally left the ground and had actually begun to fly! Oh, to be a pilot! To control such an enormous machine as this, to fly high above seas, mountains, and deserts! This was something to strive for!

Turning at a 180° angle, the plane flew over the narrow bend of seacoast known as the Gulf of Aqaba. Ten or fifteen minutes later, the stewardess Leah came out into the narrow aisle and clapped her hands to gain everyone's attention.

"Chaverim. Brothers and sisters, very shortly we'll be over the city of Eilat. This is a part of our fatherland, Israel. The remainder of this flight is over Israeli territory. Look out of the windows now if you want to catch a glimpse of Eilat."

Scarcely had she said these words before the passengers began to stir. All together they sat up on the benches again, and soon dark heads crowded around every single window.

This was to be their first glimpse of the promised land.

As it passed over Eilat, the plane flew lower and circled above the small white houses gleaming in the blinding sunlight, after which they continued in a straight line across the southern part of Israel, the Negev Desert.

At the time Shalom and his friends flew over the Negev in January of 1949, fighting between the Egyptians and the Israelis was still in progress. The stewardess didn't mention this fact to her passengers, nor did she tell them that the tents they could see here and there below were not the rude beginnings of a peaceful colony but were either Egyptian or Israeli military encampments. The Yemenite Jews were unaware that the pilots flew at a much higher altitude over the Negev to escape possible fire from the antiaircraft batallions of the Egyptians.

Soon the sun was visible only on the left side of the plane, and the people crowding about the windows on the right side saw less and less of the territory over which they were flying. The golden-white hills of Jerusalem now appeared to be dark blue. The white houses of the cities were more and more swallowed up by darkness. Nowhere below was there a light to be seen. Israel was still at war with the Arab countries, and blackouts had been in effect since the beginning of the war.

Overcome with fatigue, the travelers sat either on the benches or on the floor, and the children with their heads on their mother's knees slept as the Skymaster finally reached Lod airport and prepared for a landing. "The Lord's silver bird," the huge plane, came down with a bounce, followed by two slight bumps, at which point the wheels finally began to run smoothly across the cement runway. The din of the propellers grew quieter, and the rhythmic throb of the

motors grew slower until it died out altogether. In its present
position, the plane did indeed resemble a mighty bird with
outspread wings.

In good time the stewardess took her place at the exit and,
once she was sure the ground crew had attached the mov-
able stairway securely, opened the door. The fresh, mild
air, with just a touch of salt from the sea, streamed into the
musty atmosphere of the passengers' cabin.

"We have now landed in Israel, chaverim. May God
bless you! Come toward the door slowly and take your
turns. We have come home!"

Some of them had risen from their seats and were slowly
beginning to shuffle toward the open door when Mori
Alfeka's thin voice suddenly broke the silence.

"Stay right in your places. This woman—this shameless
creature, this immoral person, who dares to show her bare
arms and legs—has led us astray. For two thousand years we
have waited to return to the land of our fathers. And it still
isn't impossible that we will get there some day. But this is
not Israel, I tell you. This can't be the Holy Land. A long
and arduous journey awaits us before we arrive at our
destination."

The words of the elderly man caused all who had risen to
take their places again. No one moved. The stewardess
didn't know whether to laugh or cry. She was tired after her
long journey and longed to get home and go to bed. Finally
she collected herself and explained, lovingly and quietly,
that this *was* Israel, their final destination, and that she had
absolutely no desire or reason to lead her Jewish brothers
and sisters astray. But her efforts were all in vain. Still no
one would move—until suddenly one person did. Stumbling
as he made his way among the legs of the squatting pas-

sengers, Shalom struggled to reach the door. Because the red-haired Yitzhak had told him back in the settlement that the flight to Israel would take from morning to evening, he knew the stewardess was telling the truth.

Taking him by the hand, the stewardess left the plane with Shalom, and together they went into the waiting room. The girl told the head of the airport what had happened aboard the plane, but the Yemenites refused to listen to him, either. Eventually, everyone was assembled there—ground crews, police, civilian workers. Each in turn went to the door of the plane and tried to convince the immovable Marib Jews that they had to use their common sense and leave the plane, but nothing did the slightest bit of good. Someone suggested that the police would have to force the stubborn travelers to come out one by one, but this was objected to on general principles. "That would be quite a reception," a worker interrupted. "You have to remember that these are people who come from a country where life goes on as it did in the Middle Ages," another remarked.

The problem was at last solved by the head of the airport. "Send fresh water and food into them and let them sleep tonight in peace and quiet inside the airplane. We can air out the plane and clean it tomorrow morning. The chief rabbi in San'a arrived here with the first bunch of refugees, and at the moment he is living in a hotel in Tel Aviv. I'll speak with him this evening, and I'll ask him to come here as early as possible in the morning. I'm sure they'll listen to him. And now I want everyone who isn't here on official business to clear out, go his own way, and remember that this is not a laughing matter. These devout, God-fearing people are Jews. They are our brothers."

Shalom spent the night in one of the airport offices. He

slept fitfully and awakened time after time. Although he was certain he had done the right thing, he still had the nagging feeling that he should have remained with Mori Alfeka, with his mother and sister and brother, with the Marib Jews. He felt a little as if he had deserted his own people.

At dawn the next day the chief rabbi from San'a arrived at the airport, looking every inch like a prophet straight out of the Bible. When he assured the passengers that they really and truly were at their destination, they finally descended from the plane. Carefully, the men carried their most precious treasure, the parchment scrolls of the Torah.

10

All Our Beginnings Are Difficult

The Israel Shalom landed in wasn't quite equal to the dream picture he had conjured up as he lay in the hospital in El Hasched. This country, which was referred to in the Bible as a Canaan flowing with milk and honey, had, ever since the Roman legions destroyed the kingdom of Jerusalem and the Emperor Titus put an end to the Jewish state, been the site of many wars. The Byzantines followed the Romans, after which the Mongolian hordes stormed across the territory. It was here that the Crusaders fought against the troops of the Arabian caliphs and lost. The domination of the Arabs was broken by the armies of the Turkish Sultan, and for three centuries after that, the country was a poor and badly-cared-for province of the Ottoman rule. While all these wars were going on, the once-renowned irrigation system fell into disrepair, the forests were hewn down, and the Canaan flowing with milk and honey became a land of barren mountains and nonarable deserts. At the beginning of this century, a number of Jewish colonists returned to the land of their fathers to re-create, with their own bare hands, the green meadows of ancient times and to plant shade trees on the slopes. But these were few in number, and they didn't have much time to devote to their work. They managed only here and there, in the sun-

drenched terrain, to plant crops and other vegetation, which
they encircled with protective olive trees and orange groves.

The route of the bus that took the Marib Jews from the
Lod airport into the city was mainly across a deserted plain,
where the barrenness was varied only by a few sparse weeds
growing between the red ledges of rock. Now and then along
the road could be seen the remains of burned cars and tanks
that had been shot to pieces—reminders of the war that
not too long ago had raged between the attacking Arabs
and the forces of the Jews. It was January, right in the
middle of the rainy season, and gray clouds hung in the
skies.

In great disappointment Shalom looked out over the
landscape, and his state of mind was not improved when
they reached their destination, the transfer settlement called
Ros Hasyin. From all over the world emigrants had arrived
in this new Jewish state—Jews who longed to live in their
own country. But it was impossible to create housing just
by the wave of a magic wand for the thousands and tens of
thousands of newcomers. Therefore, the new inhabitants
were placed in improvised settlements. Ros Hasyin was one
of these temporary establishments. At one time the barracks
had served as shelter for British fliers during World War
II, and from the huge hangars the planes of the Royal Air
Force had taken off on many dangerous missions. The man-
ager of the settlement assigned Shalom and his group to
one of the hangars, where straw mattresses had already been
placed on the ground for the benefit of the travel-weary
Marib Jews.

"Settlements, settlements, and more settlements," Sha
lom muttered to himself. "Nothing at all to do. Just like it

was at El Hasched. Was it for this that the Skymaster, the silver bird, carried us on its back?"

However, Shalom soon realized that Ros Hasyin was not to be compared with the previous settlement. Here there was great stir and commotion around the barracks. Here more than two thousand people were living—most of whom had very recently arrived from Europe. And the Europeans certainly didn't sit around outside their quarters all day, twiddling their thumbs as the Yemenites had done in El Hasched. All day long they were busy puttering around. doing odd jobs, walking here and there, talking to one another, some friendly and some unpleasant, in languages that Shalom found utterly ununderstandable.

In addition, the officials of the settlement did everything in their power to make life in the settlement as bearable for the emigrants as possible. Scarcely had the Marib Jews made themselves at home on their straw mattresses when a small, stocky, broad-shouldered man came around and took them to the public bath. First it was the women's turn, and when they returned after an hour or so, it was almost impossible to recognize them because every one of them had been issued new clothing. Strictly speaking, the clothing was not new, because it had come from American, Swedish, and other Red Cross organizations that had collected storehouses full of used clothing, but it was, in any case, both warmer and more practical than the rags the women had brought along with them from Yemen. The women felt as if they had been born all over again in their new clothing with its unusual patterns and styles.

Shalom went along with the men to the bath, which consisted of a row of showers. Everyone undressed, and suddenly water began to stream from the showers as if on command of the broad-shouldered man. With eyes wide open, the Yemenites stared at this new miracle, and not one of them dared to get under the rushing water. But Shalom once more showed his bravery by getting under the nearest of the showers.

Once they had bathed, the men also were issued new clothing. And for them the strangest things of all were the shoes. The Yemenites, who always wore sandals and no other footwear, had never seen shoes. But here they needed both warmer clothing and heavier shoes, because in the rainy season the temperature seldom went above thirty-five or forty degrees. The Yemenites, accustomed to heat, stood around shivering. It took several days for the new-comers to get accustomed to their new environment and to get used to strange customs and rules. Electric lights were something special to them. An assistant showed them how to turn the lights on and off. In the beginning, they looked at the switch with mixed feelings of terror and respect, and the first night the lights burned all night long because no one dared to turn them off. It took the Yemenites a few weeks to accept electricity and to be able to do something about it. They were also shown how to use knives, forks, and spoons, but no one wanted to use these odd metal objects. To be sure, Shalom tried several times but quickly returned to the way he was used to eating in Marib: he drank his soup, fishing out pieces of vegetable and meat with his fingers. Anything that was left of the soup he sopped up with pieces of bread.

For the most part, the Yemenites did their best to obey the instructions of the various assistants. They learned to use soap, to wash their clothes, and to make their own beds. But there were some things they simply couldn't compre-

hend—for instance, that people should undress before they went to bed. And whenever the men were requested to go after water at the communal tap, they refused point blank. Carrying water had always been up to the women in Yemen, and no man would think of doing a woman's work.

Apart from the fact that they stubbornly refused to give up some of their own customs, the Yemenites were very little trouble in Ros Hasyin. In a good many ways, their food, sleeping quarters, and housing were better than what they had had back home in Yemen. Within a few weeks, when the rainy season had come to an end, the women were able to build their fires between two stones outside the hangar, and under the leadership of Mori Alfeka, the men could sit out in the open air and hold their endless disputes and discussions about the Holy Scriptures.

On the other hand, the Yemenites had a hard time reconciling themselves to the European refugees in the settlement. Their light complexions and hair filled them with suspicion, and they began to doubt strongly that these people were Jews at all. Their apprehensions were heightened by the fact that these "whites," as they called the Europeans among themselves, didn't observe certain customs the Yemenites held to tenaciously. The men didn't wear beards, and quite often they were bareheaded. And the women wore clothing that not only didn't cover their heads, but often also even showed their bare arms and legs. And to top it all, these heathens didn't even know Hebrew.

Mori Alfeka told his people to keep their contacts with the "whites" to an absolute minimum. Actually, his orders were somewhat superfluous, since they didn't speak the same language.

As for Shalom, he didn't pay much attention to Mori

Alfeka's instructions. As far back as the time he was in the hospital, he had found out that there were Jews with light complexions and light hair, and he had himself discovered that these "whites" knew much more about the world at large, about machines and technical things in general, than even the wisest among the Yemenites. As often as he was able, therefore, he invented errands to do at the barracks of the "whites," where he eagerly studied the lives and ways of these interesting strangers.

Faithfully, the men from Marib stuck together, prayed together, shared a common meal, and sat, between times, in a single large group at the entrance of the hangar, conversing with one another. Because of his private excursions Shalom had almost made himself a stranger to them. His people had not approved of the fact that Ingrid, with whom he had become so friendly at the hospital, had visited him several times in the settlement at El Hasched. And naturally now, everyone noticed that immediately after his meals he disappeared and made a beeline for the "whites." Perhaps they didn't say anything about all this, but it was as if they had banished him from their minds.

Shalom felt that he was being treated somewhat shabbily because his old teacher Alfeka never said a word to him, and even his own brother Yussef seemed to look straight through him without seeing him. Yet he was so occupied with studying the lives of the Europeans, with the cars that went here and there throughout the settlement, and with all the other sensations that he really didn't have time to ponder about this quiet ostracism. He was especially fond of the parking lot, where he hoped to become acquainted with one of the drivers. But the drivers were too busy to concern themselves with the shy boy from Yemen.

One day while he was strolling around the settlement, as usual, he happened to meet a boy about his own age whose name was Marcel and who, together with his parents, had come to Israel from Morocco. Marcel had no curls growing from his temple and his skin was much lighter than Shalom's, but his father had a long black beard and wore a long shirtlike costume. The Moroccan boy could speak both Hebrew and Arabic and, in addition—and this made a big impression on Shalom—French. Too, he bragged that in the Moroccan city where they had·lived he had gone to school with white boys who weren't Jewish but were Frenchmen and Christians to boot, and that he had not only ridden in an automobile but also in a train—a kind of automobile that ran on steel tracks and belched out black smoke. The latter was something Shalom didn't really believe.

As it happened, they became rather constant companions, and Marcel taught Shalom a good deal—among other things that the white Jews who had no beards and who could not speak Hebrew were called "Askenazim" and that they worshiped in quite a different way, although they recited their prayers in Hebrew.

Shalom soon realized that the Askenazim differed from the Yemenites in a good many other ways. Each morning, for example, they went to the shower room and washed themselves from top to toe, in spite of the fact that their religion demanded only that they wash their hands and their faces before praying. The living quarters of the Askenazim were always infinitely cleaner than were the hangars where the Yemenites were housed. But the Askenazim were pretty often loudmouthed and fought both among themselves and with the supervisors. And sometimes —and Shalom had seen this with his own eyes—they even had a knockdown, drag-out brawl. The children especially seemed to be regular gamecocks. One time Marcel and Shalom saw some boys kicking around a bouncy round object among themselves. They walked up to them to see what was going on. The Askenazic boys shouted something at them in their peculiar language and began to hit them. Calmly Shalom took the blows, but Marcel hit one of his aggressors in the face with his fist. A general fight ensued, and Shalom was bruised in several places, and his nose began to bleed.

The demonstration was broken up by a light-skinned Askenazic woman who hurried over to them and separated the combatants. Her intervention seemed totally incomprehensible to Shalom. How could a woman allow herself to scream at grown boys, let alone hit one of them? "Furthermore," he said to Marcel, "the men give the orders and the women are supposed to obey." Marcel assured him that this was so in Morocco, too, as far as the Jews and Arabs were concerned, but not among the French.

"Well then, are those boys and that woman French?"

"Of course not," Marcel answered contemptuously. "They can't speak a word of French. But I can!" He began to brag. "They're just white, and white people are all more or less crazy," he added with the voice of experience.

"That may be, but they can also make machines and drive cars and fly," Shalom declared.

"They aren't the only ones. In Morocco I've seen Arab and Negro drivers, let me tell you."

"Do you think anyone with skin as dark as mine could ever be a pilot?"

"Why not? Of course you can. But why? Have you thought about it?"

"I have. I spent a lot of time watching the fliers in the plane that brought us here, and I think that's a wonderful sort of work. And I know about motors and how they work," he added with a touch of bravado.

Weeks passed by in Ros Hasyin. It had gotten warmer, but otherwise nothing had changed. The European refugees more and more gave vent to their discontent, explaining angrily to the head of the settlement that they certainly hadn't come to Israel just to sit around in a transfer camp with nothing to do or to be supported by charitable organizations. Many of them took off and tried to find work on their own in the cities and villages. But those with families weren't able to leave the settlement, knowing, as they did, how hard (not to say impossible) it was to find some place to live. The state of Israel was hardly more than a year old, and the country still bore the scars of centuries of backwardness and the devastations of various wars. There would have to be an enormous amount of hard work, heavy investment, and brilliant methods of organization before there could be housing and adequate job possibilities for the thousands and tens of thousands of immigrants who had arrived.

When spring came, the heavy work began in Ros Hasyin as well. From nearby Tel Aviv came a group of factory workers, and trucks heavily loaded with spades, shovels, hoes, and other tools rolled into the large open square in the middle of the settlement. The groundskeepers gathered together those who wished to work, and within a short time there were groups of workers marching off from the settlement every morning. They cleared the settlement's fields of stones, dug ditches and the foundations of buildings under the supervision of the regular workers, mixed concrete, and broke rocks. Those who volunteered for the work received a salary for which they could buy various necessities for themselves and their families in a newly opened shop nearby. Yet very few of the Yemenites shared in the work. In part they were not particularly suited to work of this sort and were deathly afraid of the electrically powered rock crusher, and in part they felt no need to earn money. After all, they were provided with food and housing, and their requirements didn't stretch much beyond these items.

Shalom volunteered to work, but the social assistant refused to accept him.

"You're just a bit young for all this, my boy. You should go to school first, and after three or four years you can begin to work. Until that time you should be learning a good trade."

Here again it was difficult for Shalom to follow the Askenazic train of thought. In Yemen a boy of thirteen was considered fully grown. He was capable of any sort of work and could even marry if he wished. In Marib Shalom had quite often attended a wedding where the bridegroom was fourteen or fifteen years old and the bride twelve or thirteen.

The school term had begun in Ros Hasyin, but since only one teacher had been assigned from Tel Aviv, the smaller children attended school in the mornings and the older ones in the afternoon. The children were not divided into classes. The teacher wrote the letters of the Hebrew alphabet on a large blackboard, and the children copied them on a piece of paper, using the stub of a pencil. For a while Shalom was amused by writing with a pencil, but since he had long ago learned the Hebrew alphabet, could read rapidly, and had received special praise from Mori Alfeka in Marib because of his excellent handwriting, he soon became bored with sitting there in the company of the other children. Moreover, he was unhappy because the teacher taught not only boys but also girls who were allowed to attend classes here. In Marib it hadn't ever occurred to him that a girl might be taught to read and write. What good would that ever do a woman, Shalom wondered.

Most of the Yemenites shared Shalom's point of view, and the officials were not able under any conditions to get them to send their girls to school. The Yemenites, Persians, and Moroccans in Ros Hasyin became more and more convinced that the Askenazim were indeed a strange tribe.

One evening a movie was shown in Ros Hasyin. Two men from the city came to the settlement with a lot of machines, which they set up in one of the hangars. The Askenazim sat down on the benches inside, while the Yemenites squatted along the wall, silently waiting there in the darkness. Suddenly, one wall of the hangar lit up, a loud voice began to speak in a strange language, and music seemed to appear from out of the blue. On the lighted screen could be seen various figures who moved, talked, and seemed to be alive. The Yemenite women began to scream, and the men shouted, "Magic!" and "Stop this at once!" In panic they rushed out of the hangar. Never in their lives before had they heard tell of pictures that could move and speak. The first film showing was not a huge success among the Yemenites.

The next day the head of the settlement called them together, showed them the movie projector, and even handed them a small piece of film to pass around. Then the projectionist turned on the machine, and for a short while the moving figures were again seen on the screen.

The Yemenites were encouraged to go up to the screen and to feel it with their fingers. And when, the next week, there was another movie evening in Ros Hasyin, the Yemenites sat calmly and looked at the film with great interest, even if they didn't understand much of the American love story.

One morning two men and a middle-aged woman arrived at the settlement by car. They were the chairmen of a youth organization that had established special colonies—or kibbutzim—in various parts of the country where boys and girls could prepare themselves for life in Israel. Many of these youngsters were alone in the world, their parents or relatives in Europe having been the victims of Nazi atrocities. Others, like Shalom, had come to Israel from countries where the culture and civilization were centuries behind in their development.

The leaders of this youth organization wanted to recruit pupils from Ros Hasyin for a new farming colony. At the end of the working day, the head of the settlement summoned into one of the hangars all parents who had children of a suitable age. Among the Askenazim both mothers and fathers were represented, but among the Yemenites, Moroccans, and Persians, only the heads of the families showed up. They, and they alone, were able to decide the fate of their children.

Shalom's family was represented by his brother Yussef, and Shalom himself slipped in quietly just as the meeting began.

The head of the settlement made a brief speech after which he invited each one to ask whatever questions he wished. After a number of questions and answers, he asked any parents who wanted to let their children be brought up by the youth organization to register. The Yemenites displayed no great interest because they were suspicious of Askenazim in general, and the head of the settlement and the three leaders from the organization were, of course, Askenazim. But Shalom himself went up to the head of the settlement and asked to be included. When they asked him who was the head of his family, Yussef came forward and gave his permission in these words: "The family no longer takes any pleasure in him. Let him go his way."

11

In a New World

Four days later, Shalom and three other boys were driven
to the youth organization's headquarters in the city of Tel
Aviv. Tel Aviv, which is only fifty years old, was the site of
terrible fighting during the Arab-Jewish war. As they drove
along, they could see, here and there, demolished panzers
and, on the tops of the hills, ruined houses. They drove westward through a landscape marked by barren gray and
reddish-brown hills. Now and then in the gulleys they could
see a few large gardens.

"All of these trees have been planted by Jews," the youth
leader explained to the boys. "And recently we have begun
to plant crops on the slopes as well. If you go by here in
seven or eight years, you'll see that forests will be growing
on the mountainsides just as they did in Biblical times."

Just then the jeep started down a rather steep hill, and
Shalom had to hold on so as not to fall forward in his seat.
Even before the trip had started, he had begged to sit right
beside the driver so that he could see how the jeep was
handled. He watched everything the youth leader did with
the vehicle, for this interested him considerably more than
the country through which they were passing. At times he
got up enough courage to ask a few questions, such as, why
had the driver shifted gears at a particular moment? To be

sure, Yitzhak had at one time explained very carefully how
the gears worked and what they were for, but it still wasn't
perfectly clear in his mind.

In spite of Shalom's fascination with the jeep, he had
noticed that they had left the mountains behind and were
traveling across a plain. The landscape was completely different here. Growing things flourished—there were bushes,
orange groves, and wheat fields gently waving in the breeze.
At times they drove past colonies of one-story houses resembling white cubicles. All of a sudden the road curved
sharply, leading toward a suspension bridge over a narrow
but deep stream. To his astonishment, Shalom saw that the
upper part of the bridge consisted of nothing but steel con-
struction pieces that had been bent into bow-shaped forms.
It was impossible for him to imagine that a bridge could
ever be built of anything other than wood. Hardly had he
recovered from this surprise when the next one came along.
They were soon passing by rows of houses on both sides,
and from nowhere appeared a huge blue steel vehicle in
front of them. It appeared to be a kind of large bus, but
there seemed to be no room for the motor in front, and,
what was more, the vehicle ran along steel tracks. The
youth leader noticed Shalom's astonishment and enlight-
ened him by saying that the vehicle ran by means of electric
current. The information, however, left Shalom not much
the wiser.

They drove through almost the whole length of Tel Aviv
—riding on wide avenues bordered by white apartment
buildings, four and five stories high. Shalom became aware
that everyone was dressed in European clothing and that
the long costume resembling a nightshirt, which was common in Yemen, was nowhere to be seen. The women had

no hesitation in appearing on the street with uncovered arms and without veils. "Well, I guess I'll have to get used to it," Shalom said to himself. The thing he liked best was that the streets were all paved, which meant the pedestrians didn't stir up clouds of dust. The houses themselves, on the other hand, were not much to his taste. To be sure, they were clean and attractive, but they were lacking the ornaments he had seen in San'a. This must be the section where the poor people live, and they can't afford to decorate their houses, he thought.

But that wasn't really the case. When they entered the building belonging to the youth organization, Shalom was struck dumb with amazement. The floor was inlaid with gleaming, colorful, brilliant stone panels, and in every direction doors with glass panels led off to something else. The walls were painted light blue. On the ground floor they were ushered into a sort of cupboard where, after someone pushed a button, one-two-three, and they were on the third floor. A table was set for a meal in one of the rooms in expectation of their arrival.

The next morning Shalom and the youth leader continued their journey by jeep to a kibbutz called "Betar." The three other boys were already on their way to another kibbutz. Once again Shalom sat beside the driver, but this time he was a bit more aware of his surroundings. The road led along the coast; hitherto, Shalom had seen the sea only from the plane, at a height of six or seven thousand feet. The driver explained to him that this wasn't the same sea. The one he had seen from the airplane was the Red Sea, while this was called the Mediterranean. But since Shalom had never seen a map, this fact made no great impression on him. He was enchanted by the lovely blue of the water,

and his disappointment was visible when the driver told him
that the water was neither drinkable nor usable for irrigation. About noon the youth leader drove down to the shore
and said, "Now let's take a dip, Shalom." He took off his
clothes, but Shalom stood there undecided, not knowing
quite what to do. Without much enthusiasm, he fingered his
striped jersey. Meanwhile, the youth leader, having shed
the last of his garments, was already eagerly splashing
around in the water. Suddenly he took a dive and disappeared into the waves. Shalom was terrified. He was
convinced that an enormous fish must have come along and
swallowed him, just as had happened to the prophet Jonah
in the Bible. Fully dressed, he threw himself in desperation
into the water and decided that he would rescue his friend,
if possible, from the clutches of the fish. He was about
twenty or thirty yards from the shore; the water was almost
up to his chin. Suddenly the youth leader's head appeared
right beside him—out of nowhere. This frightened Shalom
even more, and he swallowed a huge gulp of the salt water.

The youth leader couldn't understand why Shalom had
thrown.himself headlong into the water fully clothed and
why he was screaming with fright. As soon as they were on
dry land, he scolded Shalom for not being more careful
of his clothes. But the clothes dried quickly in the bright
sunshine, and the jeep was soon on its way again. The road
wound along past mountains with bushes planted on the
sides and through several small communities. As they drove,
Shalom quietly told the youth leader that he had never in
his life been in water out in the open before, for the simple
reason that in Marib, where he had been born and brought
up, there had never been any opportunity to do so. He had
been unable to understand why this "white" man hadn't

sunk in the water. Whereupon the youth leader undertook
to explain to him the art of swimming, and Shalom made
up his mind to learn to swim as soon as possible.

They were in the middle of a lively discussion when they
came to Israel's largest port city, Haifa. With excited
interest, Shalom looked at the many ships in the large
semicircular bay and was especially impressed by the clouds
of smoke that were belching from one of the smokestacks.
The youth leader spoke of seafaring and ships, but down
deep in his heart Shalom decided that boats, which could
move around on the water and belch out a trail of smoke,
were probably all right but that he very much preferred
airplanes.

Haifa lies at the foot of Mount Carmel, and on the slopes
of this green mountain are a number of beautiful villas. The
jeep began to climb up the slopes of Mount Carmel in

serpentine fashion, swinging eastward a little while later,
heading for their final destination.

It was past noon when they came to a narrow side road,
on both sides of which grew huge cactuses. Out in the field
were evenly spaced rows of iron pipes. Every thirty or forty
yards, streams of water were spraying out from the pipes
and falling onto the ground close at hand. Between the pipes
could be seen the growing crops. Some distance away were
low-lying trees with silvery gray-green leaves and arched
boughs.

"Olive trees," Shalom cried out in delight, recognizing
them from Yemen. He had tasted the black or green fruits of
these trees, and he knew that when they were pressed, their
oil was excellent for cooking. In Yemen a man who owned
five or six olive trees was regarded as a rich man. And here
were whole forests of these precious trees! No doubt Israel
truly was the promised land, flowing with milk and honey—
just as it had been described in the Bible.

The driver took his foot off the gas pedal, and the jeep
took a wide, sweeping turn and came to a stop in front of a
squat white house. At the door stood a broad-shouldered
young man in khaki shorts and shirt, prepared to receive
them.

"This is Shalom Mizrachi, a newcomer from Yemen. He
has been assigned to your kibbutz. And, Shalom, this is
Moshe Ariel, the secretary of the kibbutz. I hope you are
going to be good friends."

Moshe shook hands with Shalom, and with that the
reception and the formalities of introduction came to an
end. The kibbutz secretary took them with him into a building where there was a long dining table. During the course
of the meal, Moshe and the youth leader got so deeply in-

volved in talking politics that it seemed as if they had forgotten about Shalom entirely, but Shalom didn't mind.
It gave him an opportunity to practice the use of his knife
and fork in peace and quiet and to take a look at this completely new world. He noticed that everyone at the table
was "white" and that not one had the darkish skin that was
always a sign a person had come from the Arabian countries or from Africa. This observation made him feel somewhat timid.

After the meal the youth leader took off in his jeep, and
Shalom was left alone with Moshe. The secretary was not
overly talkative and confined himself to saying that he
would begin by showing the kibbutz to Shalom. Between
some white barracks-like houses rose a huge tower, and
Moshe explained that this was the water tower of the kibbutz, which at the same time served as a watchtower. Shalom
couldn't quite understand why a kibbutz would want a
watchtower, but he was cautious and did not reveal his
ignorance by asking unnecessary questions. Not too far
away from the living quarters was a barnyard. At this time
of day it was empty: the sheep and other animals were out
grazing on the slopes. Soon they came to the fields, and
there Shalom could have a closer look at the iron pipes that
constituted the irrigation system. After the garden plots,
where they grew vegetables, came fields of ripening wheat,
which were bordered by young green trees. There was more
than a tinge of pride in Moshe's voice as he talked of
the farm work, the irrigation, and the long-awaited harvest.

While they wandered along the paths between the fields,
Shalom found out what a kibbutz was really for, and Moshe
told the story of how their kibbutz had come into being.
Five years previously a group of thirty persons had gathered

to form a farming colony. The government gave them some well-situated but dry and barren territory and a number of tools. Also, they received two cows in order to help them get started, and they were given a number of surplus military tents. They got right down to business, cleared the fields of stones, installed irrigation pipes, and with their own hands plowed up a piece of land on which they planted seed. No one received any salary, and two of the women cooked for the entire colony in the communal kitchen. With the profits from the first harvest they bought more irrigation pipes so that they could put under cultivation a still larger piece of land. The yield in the second year was so large that they could afford to build themselves a house and could abandon the tents. In similar fashion, other territories had been colonized by the Jews belonging to several hundred kibbutzim, and the desert had blossomed again.

"In a kibbutz every one of the members owns everything in common. Everyone gets the same food, each gets the clothing he needs, and everyone works to the best of his ability," Moshe explained. "You will work and learn something here, Shalom."

"Excuse me, sir, but are you the commanding officer here?"

Laughing at the question, Moshe said that there was no need to address him as "Sir." "Here we are all alike," he declared. "For one year I have been elected secretary, but next year it will be someone else's turn, and I'll return to my duties with the irrigation project. Do you understand?"

Of course Shalom didn't really understand, but he felt it would be best not to display his lack of knowledge. Several times already he had been laughed at by the "whites" because of his questions, and for this reason he had made up his mind to ask as little as possible.

The sight-seeing tour took quite a lot of time, especially since Moshe from time to time struck up conversations with the workers in the fields. Eventually, however, they headed in the direction of the dining room in order to get themselves a place at the table. There were a good many more people there now than in the middle of the day—perhaps sixty. Two young women served the food, and very shortly steaming plates of fine soup were placed in front of Moshe and Shalom, who sat side by side. When supper was over, Moshe clapped his hands several times as a sign that he wanted the floor.

"The boy at my side is Shalom Mizrachi, who came here to Israel from Yemen just a few weeks back. He has joined our kibbutz, and he seems to be a very nice fellow. I hope you'll all get along with him."

At the conclusion of Moshe's little speech, most of them left the dining hall without paying much attention to their new colleague, which hurt Shalom's pride somewhat. But eventually a man came up to the table. He was tall and somewhat bent and wore glasses.

From the first moment Shalom liked this man who took his hand, smiled amiably, and said, "My name is Rudolf Rosenbaum, and I'm the one who has to look after you young fellows here in the kibbutz. It makes me happy to have still another pupil. I've asked some of the other boys to come back here and get acquainted with you. They'll be here soon, as you will see."

Since he had a good deal of office work to get done, Moshe left them, and Rudolf began to talk with Shalom. In contrast to Moshe, the nearsighted Rudolf seemed to be very fond of talking and, especially, of asking questions.

Rudolf heard all about Yemen, about the mode of life and the customs of the Yemenite Jews, and about all the details of the long journey that Shalom and his friends had undertaken. His sharp questions impressed Shalom very much; he could see that this man with the glasses knew Yemen and its people quite well. In the course of the conversation, three boys had sat down at the table. Finally Rudolf considered the interview at an end and introduced Shalom to his three pupils.

"This fellow with the red hair is Tibor. He is two years older than you, and he's the leader of both the others. He came to Israel from Hungary during the war, together with his parents. He does fine work, and he's a whiz at soccer, but he has a fighting disposition. Be on your guard that you don't irritate him unnecessarily, because he is a quick one with his fists. We call him 'Wild Man' because it doesn't take much to throw him into a rage."

The red-haired "Wild Man" didn't seem to be bothered by the description. On the contrary, he laughed. This seemed like a peculiar reaction to Shalom. Had anyone called him "Wild Man," he would have been anything but happy. Rudolf went on with his introductions.

"And this treacherous rascal is Aaron. He was born in Poland, and he is quiet and obedient in appearance. But don't let that fool you. Actually he's as sly as a fox, and he is constantly getting into mischief. He has a good head on his shoulders, but he is maddeningly lazy. Among ourselves we call him 'Sneaker.' "

The stocky, dark-haired, broad-shouldered boy bowed politely, just as if someone had given him tremendous praise, and said in a low voice, "Thanks ever so much,

Rudolf," which made both of the others break into gales of laughter. Rudolf paid no attention to their delight and pointed to the third boy.

"Heinz, the terror of the whole kibbutz, was born in a suburb of Berlin. His father and mother are here, too, and they are fine people. I've never been able to understand how they could have hatched this monster. He does nothing but plague me with questions, and if he's able to pose a question for which I have no answer, he's beside himself with joy. He has a great supply of curiosity, sticks his freckled nose into everything, and knows it all—knows everything better than anyone else. And, strangely enough, sometimes he's right. For this reason we call him 'Wiseacre.' "

Wiseacre was a tall, strong boy with unruly blond hair. His face was covered with freckles. Shalom liked him the minute he opened his mouth. He spoke in short, declarative sentences, but his voice was extremely pleasant.

"Now, boys, I want you to pay close attention to what I have to say, for this is a serious matter," Rudolf continued. "Shalom has come to us from Yemen, a completely undeveloped corner of the world. He is not acquainted with our world, and he knows almost nothing about technical things or about modern conveniences. The color of his skin is darker than ours. Nevertheless, Shalom is our brother— a Jew just as we are—and this is his fatherland just as it is ours. Do you understand? Your duty is to teach him all the tricks and arts of everyday life as soon as possible. I will regard it as a sign of narrow-mindedness and poor character if any one of you tries to make fun of him. He is your brother, and that's the way I want you to treat him."

Wild Man, Sneaker, and Wiseacre listened to Rudolf attentively. At length, Tibor said briefly, "We understand, Rudolf." Taking Shalom with them, they walked out of the dining hall. Some distance away was a stretch of grass, toward which the boys headed. On the way Heinz the Wiseacre picked up a soccer ball from one of the houses, and soon the game was under way. Shalom took his place, and when the ball landed near him, he tried to kick it just as the others had. But he wasn't very good at it. Quite often his narrow foot simply thrust out into thin air, and even if he did manage to kick the ball, he could never make it soar into the air. It simply fell with a thud back to the ground. His friends said nothing, but Shalom was ashamed of himself anyway, especially when he missed, lost his balance, and fell flat on the ground.

The sun had set behind the distant blue mountains, and they began to find it difficult to see the ball. Rapidly the air began to cool, and the members of the kibbutz, weary from their long day's work in the heat of the sun, sat down on the benches outside the barracks. Sneaker and Wiseacre went home to visit their parents, and Wild Man and Shalom went off to the white one-story building that was the boys' dormitory. A fourth bed had already been made up in the whitewashed room, and a nightshirt had even been laid out for Shalom's use. In his locker he found a khaki shirt and a pair of shorts similar to what the others wore; there were also socks, a linen cap with an eyeshade, and a pair of heavy boots. Shalom was grateful to the officials of the kibbutz for their thoughtfulness, but he couldn't seem to muster up much real delight. In reality, he had expected a little more friendliness, and he was downcast over the fact that no one paid much attention to him and that most of the people in the kibbutz were totally unaware of his presence. It was not the first time in his life that he lay awake a long time and pondered. Perhaps it would have been better if the miracle had never happened during his lifetime, if the children of Israel had not wanted so desperately to return to the land of their fathers.

But the memory of the sufferings of the journey and all

the new impressions soon melted into nothing, and Shalom awoke to find Wild Man jerking the blankets off his bed.

Outside, everything was already in motion. Things were lively between the barracks, and things were going on in the area of the watchtower. The cows were being led out to pasture, two jeeps were already loaded with fresh vegetables that were to be taken into the market place of the nearest city, and men and women with hoes and spades over their shoulders were on their way to the fields. In the dining hall there were only a few small children and a few older people drinking milk and nibbling on the green tomatoes and olives that had been served.

After breakfast the older boys went into Rudolf's living room, which served as a schoolroom. In another of the barracks of the kibbutz the little children had their regular school classes under the direction of a younger woman teacher. But Wild Man, Wiseacre, and Sneaker had outgrown the desks in the school, and Rudolf was now in charge of them. The room was filled with books and did not resemble a classroom in the least. Many learned pedagogues would have lifted an eyebrow over Rudolf's methods of teaching. He simply sat there reading the previous day's newspaper, apparently unaware of the presence of the boys. But the minute he found something interesting, he would immediately read the article or news item aloud to them. Then a lively discussion among Rudolf and the three boys always followed, which at times almost turned into a quarrel, at which point Rudolf would take down one of his books as an aid to settling the dispute that had come up. But there were occasions on which even reference books failed to convince them, and sometimes Rudolf was forced to retire in the face of the points made by the boys.

This whole procedure was totally ununderstandable to Shalom. Up to this time he could never have imagined that a pupil could disagree with his teacher, and in addition, he felt that it was inappropriate in general to say anything in opposition to an older person. The first few days he scarcely opened his mouth, answering only when Rudolf directed questions squarely at him. He couldn't understand most of the conversation because many of the names, events, and references lacked any meaning for him. His shyness and lack of knowledge naturally didn't go unnoticed by Rudolf, but Rudolf was very careful not to lecture him or berate him in front of the other boys. About noontime, when the lessons were over, he took a book down from one of the shelves and handed it to Shalom.

"This might possibly interest you," he said. "Read it if you wish." It was a geography book, and Shalom's interest in it was so great that he had finished the book by evening. The next day when he returned the book, he got up enough courage to ask for another. This time it was a book of ancient history.

Rudolf made no comment on his diligence but acted as if it were the most natural thing in the world that a boy would absorb a textbook in just a couple of evenings. When the discussions led to questions that had anything to do with the reading in which Shalom was engaged, Rudolf would ask him a question. And if, for example, Shalom could then answer that London was the capital of England or that in Roman times Spain was called Hispania, Rudolf would nod approvingly.

At times Rudolf took his violin out of the case and played something for the boys. Following these spur-of-the-moment concerts, there were lively discussions about Mozart, Beethoven, or various modern composers. On another occasion, Rudolf handed the boys paper and pencils, and the boys figured out together what percentage of the yearly budget of the kibbutz could be set aside for the amortization of the loan and what percentage could be used to buy new irrigation pipes. Without actually being aware of it, Shalom learned an enormous amount from Rudolf and from the books he was permitted to borrow. The mornings and the hours that followed supper were the happiest times for Shalom. The afternoons, which the boys spent working, appealed to him much less. They had to clear stones from the land that was planned for fields, break up the clods of earth around the plants, or hoe down weeds, unless they were assigned to spraying fruit trees or helping to clean out the barnyard. The secretary of the kibbutz informed Rudolf every morning the place where the boys were supposed to work after lunch or which part of the kibbutz was most in need of their help.

To begin with, Shalom felt that working in the fields was very strenuous, but as the days passed into weeks, his body became accustomed to it. The thing that bothered him more than the actual labor itself was that it all seemed so monotonous. They all talked to one another as they worked, mentioning in passing every imaginable everyday thing, and sometimes they would sing a song if the work were of a lighter sort. For his part, Shalom didn't join in either the conversations or the singing. He just dreamed of how much nicer it would be to go off somewhere in the shade with a book or to talk to Rudolf about what he had been reading.

As was the case everywhere in Israel, Saturday was a day of rest at the kibbutz. Before the Friday evening meal, everyone changed into clean clothes, after which they assembled at the base of the watchtower. A campfire was lighted, which took away the chill of the evening, someone would take out an accordion or Rudolf would go after his fiddle, and then the young people began to dance. In a huge circle, hand in hand, they danced the ancient Jewish hora. Many times they invited Shalom to join them, but he wanted no part of it. When there was community singing, Shalom remained silent, partly because he didn't know the songs and partly because he didn't have an especially resonant voice. At times someone would recite a poem, and sometimes there were movies in the dining hall, which Shalom enjoyed very much, but otherwise Friday evenings struck him as rather boring and hard to live through.

At first the boys did their level best to make friends with Shalom, but when they noticed that he didn't display any great enthusiasm for soccer, shot-putting, or broad-jumping, they paid less and less attention to him. Shalom felt that he wasn't especially welcome, but he didn't seem to realize that it was mainly his own fault. He could not act freely and easily with his comrades, and in addition, he was perhaps a little afraid of them because he had noticed they had nothing against a knockdown, drag-out fight. They had boxing matches in which they tried to beat each other up, also. Shalom felt more and more that he was being overlooked. He had no way of knowing that Wild Man, Wiseacre, and Sneaker had many times discussed the subject of Shalom with Rudolf and that each time Rudolf had advised them not to disturb the newcomer. "Let him alone until he has grown into his new clothes and learned to be a part of us. You'll see. One of these days he'll be a good colleague and friend, after he really begins to feel at home here. Don't bother him if he wants to be left in peace," Rudolf told the boys, who, in turn, followed his advice.

But Shalom knew nothing of this. And in addition, he was unaware of the fact that Rudolf had told the other members of the kibbutz that Shalom caught onto things rapidly and that he had a razor-sharp intellect. The others began to regard him with a certain appreciation, and they thought that he was a diligent, pleasant fellow. But Shalom, on the other hand, felt more and more that no one could be bothered with him and that at times they out and out despised him. He directed all of his attention and affection toward Rudolf, and the other members of the kibbutz remained strangers to him, just as he himself felt strange and left out.

At night, when the lights had been turned out, he often lay wondering if he had done the wrong thing in joining the kibbutz in company with all these strangers. Perhaps he would have been better off if he had remained with his family, with the Jews from Marib, even if his brother and Mori Alfeka bore their grudges against him. In addition, he missed his mother and sister desperately, and the little news he had of them only made him more aware of his homesickness.

"But if I had stayed there with the Marib Jews, I would never in my life have a chance to be a flier," he said at the end of every discussion he had with himself.

12

Three Steps Forward and Two Steps Back

The weeks and months went by quickly. Nothing unusual happened in the kibbutz, but with every passing day Shalom became more accustomed to his new way of life and all that it involved. He had grown used to the work, which, in the beginning, had seemed so strenuous, was able to understand more and more of the discussions in Rudolf's room in the mornings, and began to like the food in the dining hall, though at first he had found it almost inedible. Without being especially aware of it, he began to fit into the life of the kibbutz and to feel the same enthusiasm as the others when the secretary, at the weekly meeting, reported the purchase of cotton plants, which meant that they could begin to cultivate a cotton crop on the fields that had recently been cleared of stones. He was as unhappy as the others when their best milk cow got sick, and he eagerly awaited the visit of the veterinarian from the city.

He himself was not conscious of how much he had adjusted to his new surroundings. He still felt that he was a stranger among strangers, among people with customs that seemed unfathomable to him, although he did his best to behave tolerantly. It still seemed to him that no one bothered about him. He was therefore amazed one afternoon, when they were sawing dry branches from an orange

135

tree, to hear Moshe say to him, "Come and see me in the office after supper, Shalom. There's something I'd like very much to talk to you about."

For the remainder of the working hours, he wondered what Moshe wanted. They hadn't exchanged more than a few remarks since he had arrived at the kibbutz. His sense of curiosity nagged at him so much that he did an unusual thing: he turned to Wild Man who was working alongside him and asked, "Why do you suppose Moshe asked me to come to the office?"

"Oh, didn't you know? There's going to be an election soon now," his companion said in great seriousness. "And I'll tell you a secret. The kibbutz has picked you as its candidate for parliament. And now Moshe wants to tell you how to advise Premier Ben-Gurion when you get to be a member of parliament."

The people working nearby couldn't help breaking into laughter as they listened to the conversation. They appreciated the joke Wild Man was making and knew how absurd it was to think of this small, thin boy, who had been in Israel for just a few months, as an adviser for the father of their country, Ben-Gurion.

But, alas, Shalom had no sense of humor. He felt they were all making fun of him, and suddenly he was white with anger. Casting aside the tool he held in his hand, he quickly stepped up to his tormentor. His fist shot out straight toward Wild Man's chin. Whether it was because of the strength of the blow or the unexpectedness of it, no one could tell, but suddenly the red-haired boy was flat on the ground. Shalom hadn't knocked him out, however, and almost immediately Wild Man was on his feet again, pounding vigorously at Shalom's stomach. There was no doubt the fight would

have ended with Wild Man the victor if it hadn't been stopped in the early stages. The people around quickly separated the combatants. The fighting was stifled almost before it had begun.

Everyone returned to his duties, but to be on the safe side, Shalom chose the tree farthest away from Wild Man. His sudden outbreak of wrath had been cooled by the physical exertion, and now he was ashamed that he had given vent to his emotions. Moreover, he was more than a little afraid that Wild Man would seek revenge. The beating that he could almost surely count on was not an attractive prospect, and for another thing, he had begun to think that he must have appeared totally impossible to his comrades and that he would certainly get a scolding from Rudolf. He didn't doubt for a moment that Wild Man would tell Rudolf about their fight.

At suppertime Shalom tried to sit at another table, but Rudolf called to him and made him sit in his usual place— right beside Rudolf himself. Shalom didn't once lift his eyes from his plate, but he noticed, nevertheless, that Wild Man, Wiseacre, and Sneaker never took their eyes off him and that there was nothing of a friendly nature in their glances.

As soon as he had eaten, he rushed out toward the office so that, at least for the moment, he could escape meeting his adversaries. On the way to the office, he was struck with an idea. Bending down, he picked up a number of large rocks and carefully put them in his pants pockets. "If anyone attacks me, I'll hit the first one who dares in the head with a stone," he said to himself.

Moshe sat behind his desk, which was totally covered with papers. Half mumbling to himself, he was adding up long columns of figures. He motioned to Shalom to sit down but continued to mumble and chew on his pencil. Finally he finished his work and turned to Shalom.

"As you know, Shalom, it will soon be time for the high holidays of the fall season here—Rosh Hashanah and Yom Kippur. On these occasions, Jewish families like to be together. It has been a number of months now since you saw your family, and we decided that perhaps you'd like to pay them a visit. Naturally, the kibbutz will pay your traveling expenses, and you can even have a little pocket money so that you can buy a New Year's present for your mother. The only question is—do you yourself want to make the trip or would you rather spend the holidays here with us?"

"Oh, do I ever want to make the trip!" Shalom replied. Was it genuinely possible that he would get to see his mother and sister, to eat his mother's good food again? In the face of this attractive invitation, he even regarded his brother as a loved one, not as the strict head of the family.

"Well, that's fine, Shalom," Moshe said with a smile. "If you want to, you can ride in to the city in the jeep tomorrow, and before night falls, you'll be warming your hands over your own hearth. You have ten days' leave. And we send our best New Year's greetings to your whole family."

The sheer delight of it all made Shalom do the crow hop from the office to the watchtower, but suddenly he stopped in his tracks. Not more than twenty yards from him stood Wild Man gesticulating violently and saying something to the other boys.

"I'll bet they're deciding to beat me up," Shalom mused bitterly. Just to be on the safe side, he walked in a wide arc to the left and joined a smaller group who stood nearby smoking and discussing something. Although he was stand-

ing right beside them, he actually didn't catch what they
were talking about because his entire attention was directed
to the right. Wild Man was still talking vehemently to
Sneaker and Wiseacre, both of whom nodded in agreement.
In order to seem more confident, Shalom stuffed his hands
into his pockets and assured himself that the rocks were still
there. A few moments later the boys disappeared, but the
noises coming from the direction of the football field made
it clear as to just what they were up to. Scurrying to the
dormitory, Shalom picked up the book that he had bor-
rowed from Rudolf the day before. With book in hand, he
made a beeline for his favorite place—the well-lighted stairway leading to the dining hall. He tried to concentrate on his
reading, but no matter how hard he tried, he couldn't keep
his mind on it. His thoughts jumped from the forthcoming
trip to his mother and sister and brother, to the fight he had
gotten into that afternoon. At this point he felt deeply
regretful—almost ashamed—of his actions. When it came
right down to it, Wild Man was a nice fellow who always helped him out whenever he could, and now they were
going to be enemies for life. Furthermore, Shalom still had
a beating coming to him.

It grew late. The light at the entrance to the dining hall
was turned out, and Shalom felt goose pimples on his back
as the night wind began to blow. He made a quick decision
to head for the dormitory. "I'll just let things happen as they
will," he said to himself. "We'd better get the whole thing
cleared up."

Wild Man and Sneaker had already gone to bed, and
Wiseacre was sitting on the edge of his, taking off his shoes.
Without a word Shalom entered the room and walked over

to his bed. The silence made him nervous, but he tried valiantly not to show it.

At length Wiseacre said, "Rudolf told us that you're going home to visit your family for ten days starting tomorrow. It's a shame that you won't be with us here for the holidays, because we usually celebrate them nicely. And the food is unusually good. Chicken with tomato sauce. Mmmmmmmm!"

"You goof. You think of nothing but your stomach," came a sudden retort from Sneaker, who had obviously not yet fallen asleep. "Shalom will have a wonderful time at home with his family, and I'm sure they have lots of good food there for the holidays, too. What did you usually have for Rosh Hashanah at home in Yemen, Shalom?"

"Porridge with melted butter and honey," Shalom answered. His voice was barely audible.

"There, you see! You're an idiot," Sneaker said to Wiseacre. "Doesn't that sound good? I think porridge is great, and when you have honey on it . . ."

"Hey! Turn out the lights because I want to go to sleep," Wild Man said in a loud voice. "We can argue about chicken and porridge with honey tomorrow morning!"

Shalom lay in his bed expecting the attack to begin any minute. He waited and waited, holding fast to the rocks under his pillow. But absolutely nothing happened. Breathing heavily, Sneaker and Wiseacre were clearly asleep, and Wild Man was snoring softly, just as he did every night.

The next morning Shalom put on clean clothes, rolled up his nightshirt, toothbrush, and soap, and then waited outside the dormitory for the jeep to drive him to the city. The car from the settlement was almost at the door when Wild Man came out and began to talk to Shalom.

"Hey, Shalom. You're just about to take off on a long

trip, and it's not a good idea to be unprepared in case something should happen. I thought maybe you'd better take this
with you. You can have it as a New Year's present from
me." He handed Shalom a scout knife in its leather case,
the knife he had always worn in his belt and of which he was
very proud.

Shalom reached out his hand but, in his astonishment,
was totally unable to make the Hebrew words, "todah rab-
bah"—"thank you"—come out. By this time the jeep had
stopped, and Moshe, who had been sitting beside the driver,
hopped out.

"We're giving you some pocket money, Shalom. Ten
pounds. Avram the driver will buy your bus ticket for you.
And please give this package to your mother. It contains a
little sugar, some raisins, and nuts. The kibbutz sends its
best New Year's wishes to your whole family. And we'll
expect you back, healthy and happy, when the holidays are
over." Shalom was amazed at all this thoughtfulness.
Hadn't he believed that no one in the kibbutz paid any attention to him?

Soon the jeep was rolling down the dusty country road.
The three boys, Moshe, and Rudolf, who stood there waving
good-by to him, became smaller and smaller. But in his
mind he could still hear their voices wishing him a nice trip
and a fine time over the holidays.

Once in the city, they found a long line waiting for the bus
to Beersheba, the place where Shalom was to go. All of the
Jews from Marib, including the Mizrachi family, had found
work and places to live in the ancient city, mentioned so
often in the Bible, which the present-day Jews had awakened
to new life. Beersheba lies at the northern edge of the huge
Negev Desert. Eager hands had planted trees and quick-

growing eucalyptus bushes all around the modern white apartment buildings that lined both sides of the streets in the new part of the city.

But Shalom was going to have several hours in the crowded bus before he reached his destination. Fortunately, he had a window seat and was able to enjoy the wonderful view off toward the mountains of Galilee. The road led down to the south, and the terrain grew flatter and flatter. The landscape became rather monotonous, and the heat was more oppressive here than up in the mountains.

Again and again the bus passed groups of workers. It was a tedious, difficult job to build stone terraces on the slopes. Mules were carrying huge baskets full of humus, which would be used to fill in the terraces. "Soon there will be fruit trees blossoming all over this barren ground," explained an older man who was sitting beside Shalom. On the flatlands, tractors were plowing up the ground that had been so dried out by the sun, and here and there irrigation pipes were being laid. At the edge of one village, women were singing as they joyfully harvested the olives. During the whole trip there was much to see, and Shalom was almost disappointed when the journey came to an end and the bus turned in at the large square in Beersheba.

The bus conductor explained to Shalom where he would have to go in order to get to the new colony where the Yemenite Jews lived. It didn't take ten minutes for him to reach a group of white two-story houses. In every building there were four apartments, and the straight streets were bordered by young trees that clearly had been planted only a few months ago. Little children were playing in the dust of the streets, several larger boys were kicking a soccer ball, and a number of hens were scratching around in the scorched yellow grass that grew near the walls of the houses. It was easy to see that the houses were brand-new, and it was equally obvious that the inhabitants had not yet become accustomed to life in a modern city or to modern times. In many of the windows washing was hung out to dry, and from many kitchens a regular cloud of smoke poured out. In the street lay scraps of paper and fruit peelings.

Shalom felt a bit gloomy as he saw this lack of order. He had forgotten that the streets in Marib, both in the Jewish and Arab quarters, looked just like these. But he had grown accustomed to neatness and cleanliness in the kibbutz, where you never threw scraps of paper into the street or poured out your dishwater just any old place, and small children were certainly not allowed to run around half naked in the dust.

In a little two-room unit, Shalom was received with much joy by his mother and sister. Time after time his mother dried her eyes with a corner of her apron—and it was anything but clean. "I can't get over how you've grown since I saw you last, my son!" she repeated. Soon his brother arrived. He, as well as a number of the other Marib Jews, worked in a textile factory in the neighborhood. Even Yussef seemed glad to see Shalom, and he had apparently forgotten that they had not parted in the friendliest of ways.

Shalom had tears in his eyes, caused less by emotion than by the smoke that filled the kitchen. Though the window was open, the room was not aired out. Shalom realized that his mother was in the middle of her cooking and that the cooking was being done on an open fire in the middle of the kitchen floor. The improvised open fireplace consisted of four bricks, over which had been placed a huge iron kettle. There was a stove in the kitchen, but it stood cold and unused. "Why?" Shalom asked his mother. "Why do you insist on making a fire on the floor when there's a perfectly good stove here?"

"I don't understand these new metal stoves, my son," his mother explained. "The fire just goes out. And I get so tired standing in front of it. You know that back in Marib we always made a fire on the floor, and it's very difficult to change your old habits."

In the "living" room Shalom saw a strange sight. The colony committee had given the new tenants tables and chairs, beds, and cupboards for their apartments. There were also two low cupboards along the wall, on top of which the chairs had been placed, upside down. The table was off in one corner, and the room seemed almost empty of furniture. Shalom found in the kitchen what was obviously the remains of one of the beds. It had been cut up for firewood.

Shalom's mother hastened to explain that, too.

"We don't want anything to do with beds, my boy. I tried to sleep in one but didn't sleep a wink the whole night because I was so afraid of falling off. And your brother didn't like sleeping so high, either. Therefore, we have burned up one bed after the other—they burned just fine for that matter—and we sleep on our mats, just as in Marib. And the chairs? You ask why they're on the cupboards? Well, that's where they were when we got the apartment. And naturally nobody wants to sit on them. They're too uncomfortable."

Shalom said nothing. He realized that whatever he might say would be useless. They ate their evening meal sitting on the floor, without knife or fork, and they scooped kidney beans with melted butter from a common dish. Shalom didn't want to admit, not even to himself, that his mother's cooking wasn't perhaps as tasty as the food he had now become used to at the kibbutz. He no longer liked eating out of a common bowl. But certainly it was wonderful to spend an evening in his family circle, and this made him very happy.

The next day, the eve of the holidays, the Marib Jews began, as early as midafternoon, to assemble outside the building where one of the apartments had been converted into a house of prayer. There was a lovely modern synagogue in the city, but the Yemenites never went there, mainly because the order of the services and the melodies of the psalms weren't in accordance with their traditions. And naturally the officials had nothing against letting the newcomers from Yemen keep to their own house of prayer.

On the shady side of the house sat Mori Alfeka, squatting down and leaning his back against the wall. He was surrounded by the heads of the families. The only difference was that they were no longer dressed in their long garments but in linen slacks and shirts. In addition, most of them were smoking—something they had learned from the Askenazim. But the faces, most of the beards, and their movements were completely unchanged, and there had been no noticeable alteration in their manner of conversation.

Following Yemenite tradition, Shalom greeted his old teacher and the heads of the Marib Jewish families with three deep bows, and they returned his greeting by lifting their hands to their foreheads. Mori Alfeka invited Shalom to take a place in the circle—a great distinction since he was not the head of any family. Following this little ceremony, Mori Alfeka continued the conversation, or, rather, the lecture of enlightenment.

"It was a mistake, a great mistake, my brethren, for us

to have left the city of our birth, Marib, in the belief that God had sent us the Messiah. The Messiah has not yet come to us, and we must still wait upon the mercy of God. All of our sufferings and indignations stem from the fact that the Messiah has not appeared. We must wait, my brethren, just wait," he ended in complaint.

Forgetful of the fact that he really had no voice in the congregation, Shalom, used to the morning classes with Rudolf and the boys, posed a quick question, which he directed to Mori Alfeka.

"What do you mean—sufferings and indignations? What sufferings are you forced to endure here?"

The heads of the families, and especially Shalom's brother, glanced angrily at this boy who had dared to go against the ancient, unwritten law, but Mori Alfeka realized what had happened and waved deprecatingly.

"Let the boy alone, my brethren. We suffer from all the unbelief that swarms about us. The Askenazim shave off their beards, their women run around in short skirts, and they make fires on the Sabbath day. They go so far as to ride in cars on the holy days, and in the hospitals the doctors and nurses work, and in still other places the people break the law which states that no one may do any work on the Sabbath. And above all, my son Shalom, we must still bear the curse put upon mankind when it was driven out of paradise: 'Hereafter you shall earn your bread by the sweat of your brow . . .' "

Shalom was bowled over. He couldn't help asking, "Do you believe that we won't have to work any more when the Messiah does come? Why, here we work in our own country, work for our own people. Human beings can't exist without work. Work is a part of our very lives . . ."

"When the Messiah comes, no one on earth will have to work any longer. I can see, my son, that even you have been corrupted by the Askenazim and have adopted their customs. You have gotten rid of the curl at your temples, and you wear short pants." Sorrowfully, Mori Alfeka shook his head to lend added emphasis to his words.

Shalom knew that there wasn't anything more to say and that any argument he might come up with would be rejected by the old men and the heads of the families who sat there, crouched against the wall, agreeing with Mori, who represented an ancient mode of life, filled with deep belief and poetry—but, unfortunately, a way of life that was incompatible with modern times. A conviction of this sort, so deeply rooted, can be shaken neither by facts nor arguments.

The first star was visible in the heavens, the sign, according to Jewish tradition, that it was time for evening services to begin. Stiff-legged, and moving like an old, old man, Mori Alfeka arose and went into the house of prayer, followed at a respectful distance by the others. Inside the house of prayer, everything was just as it had been in Marib. Mori Alfeka, as the leader, took his place on a platform in the middle of the room. Two wax candles burned, one on either side of the ark of the covenant with the Torah scrolls, and the congregation sat down cross-legged on the benches along the walls. The white prayer shawls, bordered in blue, came out, and all the heads were covered. The women's place was in an adjoining room, because, according to Biblical tradition, men alone could enter the house of prayer. Suddenly stillness descended on the little synagogue. No one made the slightest movement, and from the platform could be heard the quaking, elderly voice of Mori Alfeka as he began the holiday prayer.

"Blessed be our Lord God, Creator of the World, the Eternal God who has granted us this day!"

Shalom neither could nor wanted to escape from the pious mood of the services. He recited his prayers and sang the beautiful psalms of King David along with the others. But when services were over and he was back at home sitting in the family circle and eating the holiday food, the porridge heavy with melted butter and honey, he felt a vague longing for Rudolf, the three boys, Moshe, and the life in the kibbutz in general.

Ten days' leave can go so quickly. Every morning Shalom took a walk to the center of the city to observe the carts that came into the square with farm products from the nearby villages, and the Bedouins on their camels who came to the city to lay in supplies. With the money Moshe had given him, he bought some modest presents in one of the shops for his mother and sister, and even his brother was favored with an aluminum cigarette case. He found the life in this bustling, growing city very diverting. In the afternoons he read the newspapers or went on expeditions to the cultural center, where there was a library with a cool reading room.

At the end of his leave, he hopped off the bus and walked over to the waiting jeep, greeting the driver Avram with such exuberance that he must have been amazed.

Late in the afternoon they arrived at the kibbutz. The colony seemed completely deserted; obviously, everyone was out in the fields. Only from the kitchen, where the evening meal was in preparation, could you hear any banging or talk. Shalom went up to his room and, for a few minutes, revelled in the neatness and cleanness of the room and the serious, dedicated atmosphere that prevailed within the whole kibbutz.

At the evening meal he was reunited with Rudolf, Wild Man, Wiseacre, and Sneaker, who greeted him happily, heartily, and warmly.

"We were actually afraid that you would never come back to us, because we were convinced that you'd find you preferred porridge with honey to vegetable soup and spaghetti with grated cheese."

The latter was being served that evening, and Shalom disproved Rudolf's gloomy predictions by displaying a ravenous appetite, the result of his having gotten terribly hungry on the trip. After the evening meal, all five of them sat down on a bench under a palm tree, and Shalom told them from beginning to end everything he had seen and experienced during the trip and his visit at home. He had no wish to speak ill of his family or of the Marib Jews, but in carefully chosen words he managed to convey, in any case, vivid pictures of all that had happened, halting especially as he described the scene in the yard outside the house of prayer. As he told of Mori Alfeka's great complaints, the other boys began to giggle, but Rudolf said very solemnly:

"This is a serious thing, boys, and nothing to laugh about. It is that stubborn tenacity to religion and the ancient customs that has made Judaism possible for two thousand years in the midst of a non-Jewish environment. It's evident now that the ancient rules for living won't do as a basis for life in a modern country such as Israel is today. But you can't expect that people who have grown up in that belief, who have felt it to be the center of their existence, can throw it off from one day to the next now that they've come to Israel. We have to treat all this with patience, with gentle understanding, and, above all, with love. The second generation will be able to reconcile themselves much more easily to the reality of life in Israel."

Shalom felt deep gratitude for Rudolf's words. Perhaps Rudolf wasn't aware that his words constituted the answer to a question that had haunted Shalom ever since he arrived in Israel: "Is it right of me to divorce myself from the Marib Jews, to accept and take on the way of life of the Askenazim?" But as a result of Rudolf's wise, sympathetic words, he knew that he had done the right thing, and this knowledge comforted him. The nagging, small, ever-present feeling of self-reproach was suddenly gone with the wind, and he knew now how he must handle his relationships with his family and the other Marib Jews. Love and understanding —even if he couldn't bring himself to share their concepts of life or customs—were the rules according to which he must behave.

The next morning there was a big surprise awaiting Shalom in Rudolf's room—a girl about his own age.

"Katrine," Rudolf said to the girl, "here is the fellow we've all been talking about. Shake hands with your new colleague, Shalom."

With a slight feeling of hesitation, Shalom followed the request, hesitant because he wasn't used to shaking hands with girls. While Rudolf explained to him that Kati and her parents had only recently come to Israel from Stockholm, the capital of Sweden, and that the family had been absorbed into the kibbutz, Shalom took a good look at the girl. She had chestnut-brown hair and big gray eyes, and there were a few freckles around her nose. But in spite of the freckles, or maybe because of them, she seemed very attractive. Freely she smiled at Shalom, displaying a row of large but very lovely teeth.

"Kati will be studying with us in the morning classes, Shalom. As yet she can't speak much Hebrew since she's had only a couple of months of it, but in general she knows more than the rest of you put together. Shalom, you'll have to help Kati with the language. But now let's take a look at the newspaper. Here on the first page is an article about anti-British demonstrations in Burma. Who knows anything about Burma? Maybe it's best that we take out the map right away . . ."

That morning differed from the previous mornings only in that Rudolf now and then addressed a question to Kati and corrected her at times when her grammar was wrong. Wild Man, Sneaker, and Wiseacre seemed to have become accustomed to her presence and didn't seem disturbed by the fact that a girl had joined in what had been a masculine circle, but Shalom felt this to be highly unusual, and he couldn't seem to get back into the swing of things. After lunch, when they were on their way to work in the fields, he asked the boys what they thought of Kati.

"She seems very nice," Wiseacre said approvingly. "She doesn't disturb anybody, and that's the most important thing."

"I think she's fine," Sneaker agreed. "In the afternoon she works in the sewing room. And she plays the piano very well, too. On one of the evenings during the holidays, she played Mozart and Chopin for us after supper. And she's not always acting as most women usually do. But of course she can't play soccer. What a shame!"

Wild Man didn't enter into the conversation but stayed instead at the edge of the group. Evidently he was occupied with many things other than the personality or qualities of the new girl. They had almost gotten to the new field when he said, "Look, we're going to have a meeting this evening. Come into the dormitory after supper, all of you, because we have to discuss our plan with Shalom."

13

The Big Plan

They sat in their room, each on the edge of his own bed, and it was Wild Man who led off.

"While you were on leave, Shalom, Rudolf read a very interesting article from the newspaper one morning. In a cave in the mountains near the Dead Sea, two Arabian shepherd boys found some stone jars that contained parchment scrolls. In one way or another, the scrolls finally reached the hands of some archaeologists at the Hebrew University in Jerusalem, and they found out that they dated from the time just shortly before the birth of Christ. It was the members of a sect called the Essene Jews who had recorded their deeds in books, which they kept in jars, and who had hidden them in the cave. Probably to protect them from their enemies. One of the scrolls was one of the books of the Bible."

At this point Shalom interrupted briefly, and somewhat impatiently, because he didn't really understand why all this had to be discussed at a special meeting.

"Take it easy, Shalom, and you'll soon have an explanation of the whole thing," Wild Man declared. "You're absolutely right that there are thousands of books and parchment scrolls with texts from the Bible. But this scroll is apparently the oldest manuscript of any of the books of the

Bible hitherto discovered. That was what Rudolf said, and he certainly must understand the situation. And then he said, too, that the remainder of the scrolls would illuminate what up to now has been a fairly unknown and important period in the history of mankind."

"I see," said Shalom. "But tell me what we personally have to do with these scrolls."

"They concern us a great deal," said Wiseacre, taking the floor. "If they have found such important and priceless things in the caves near the Dead Sea, we can surmise that the old Jews hid their records or other things of great worth in the caves up around here too. Rudolf told us that in ancient times it was the custom, during wars or other times of danger, to hide all precious possessions. Maybe some of these people died in the war, and what they had hidden remained there, because of course there was no one left who knew where to dig the stuff out."

"Just a minute. I can tell you that people talked about old buried treasure and all that in Yemen, too. But"—and here Shalom laughed aloud—"someone has yet to find any of the treasures. It's all just a bunch of talk . . ."

"But the parchment scrolls that were found near the Dead Sea were not just talk. We're not thinking about finding buried treasure. These would be archaeological finds," Sneaker said stubbornly.

"And may I ask where you expect to find any caves on the kibbutz's property? I haven't seen one. Or were you perhaps thinking of taking a trip down to the Dead Sea?" Shalom asked ironically.

"You're right in saying that there aren't any caves on our property," Wild Man admitted. "And we certainly didn't have in mind going down to the Dead Sea, either, because

the place is flooded with archaeologists, and they're much
better equipped than we. But not far away from here is a
chain of mountains, and there are lots of caves there. You
can see the mouths of the caves clearly with the binoculars
if you're up on top of the watchtower. The only trouble is
that the chain of mountains lies on the other side of the
border, over there in Arab territory."

"On Arab territory!" Shalom exclaimed, appalled. "You
know good and well how often we've been told that it's
strictly forbidden to go near the border. The Arabs make
quick work of anyone they catch on their side. Just three
weeks ago, machine-gun shot came from a position on the
mountains because someone had happened to get too close
to the posts at the border. You can't mean that you want
to go over there."

"That's exactly what we have in mind," Wild Man explained impassively. "And if we happen to find anything in
the caves, we will not only have done archaeology a good
turn but also the kibbutz. The Arabian shepherd boys got a
huge reward because they found the scrolls and turned them
over to the authorities. If we find something, maybe the
kibbutz can buy a whole bunch of new water pipes with
the money."

"And maybe they can at last construct a real soccer field.
And buy soccer boots for us," Sneaker added hopefully.

"But if you think the whole thing is too much of a risk,
just say so. There's nobody who's making you come along
with us," Wild Man interjected.

Shalom felt the blood rising to his head. Why would they
think that he would be any more afraid than anyone else?
Simply because his skin was darker or because they didn't
have cars or movies in Yemen? He was just about to bark

out an answer, but at the last moment he bit his lips and kept silent. Three pairs of eyes looked questioningly at him. A second later Shalom, in full control of himself, answered.

"Oh, yes, I'm with you. But I want to know a little more about the whole thing. Tell me what Rudolf thinks about it."

All three of them began to talk at once, but at length Wild Man managed to silence both of the others. As Shalom had suspected, no one in the kibbutz knew of the boys' plan.

"And nobody's going to know about it, either," Wild Man said firmly. "If you squeal on us, we'll never speak to you again. Rudolf of course would report the matter to Moshe, the secretary, right away, and then we'd get not only a big chewing out, but we might also be expelled from the kibbutz altogether. You know that there's all this talk about our fostering possibilities for peaceful coexistence with the Arabs, about how we can't provoke them, and all. Just as if the Arabs would keep calm if no one ever bothered them . . ."

"I understand that the plan is a secret," Shalom declared. "But how do you think you can manage all this without help?"

In lieu of an answer, Wild Man produced a map of the kibbutz and the territory around it. On the map someone had already drawn a red line from the watchtower of the kibbutz to a point on the mountains on the Arab side. Wiseacre, the one among the boys who was best equipped to deal with maps, explained to Shalom that the somewhat uneven line represented their proposed route. At the point where the line reached the mountain, the mouth of the largest cave was located. It came out that the boys had climbed up the watchtower every time Rudolf was on guard duty and, under the pretext of studying their geography, had also studied the territory very carefully with the aid of binoculars. The line on the map was the result of their observations.

"There's a wadi that runs right along the border," Wiseacre explained. "It's a deep river bed, and the water runs down into it from the mountains during the rainy season. As long as we stick to the river bed, no one can see us either from the Arab village or from the kibbutz. The troubles will begin when we have to take leave of the wadi, because from there we have to go about a mile in completely open territory. There aren't any trees or bushes, and the territory is very easy to observe from both sides. But once we've crossed that open stretch, we can hide behind rocks on the mountains."

Wiseacre was pretty sleepy, but Shalom didn't feel like going to bed at all. At first he had thought that the plan wasn't very well thought out, but now that he had heard a few more details, the whole thing interested him more the longer they sat there discussing the various difficulties. Wild Man had obviously thought it all through and solved all the problems—at least in theory. In the first place, they needed clothing that would be very much like the clothing of the Arab boys on the other side—that is, shirtlike garments that came clear down to the ground. Wild Man suggested that their nightshirts would do for the purpose, if they were longer, and that was something Kati might be able to help them with.

"Kati works in the sewing room. All we need to do is tell her that we're freezing to death in our short nightshirts now that the rainy season is almost upon us and the nights are beginning to be cooler. We'll ask her to sew a piece about nine inches long on the tails of our nightshirts. She's

SCHROED
E,
L N

Pickup by:
11/17/2023

7876

a nice girl, and I'm sure she won't refuse us these small favors."

They decided that their expedition should get under way right after lunch on a Saturday afternoon. They didn't have to work on Saturdays, which meant that there was no one in the fields after lunch and that they would have six long hours at their disposition before supper. According to Wild Man's calculations, it would take them two hours and a half to get to the grotto and back, and that way they would have almost four hours to devote to their cave research.

"We'll have to take spades and hoes with us," Wild Man declared, "but that's a simple matter, because we'll just take a few of them from the settlement. We'll have to content ourselves with tools that have short handles and that we can hide under our shirts—because it's important that we don't look suspicious in case the Arabs catch sight of us. There are Arab military people stationed in the village, you see, and we're taking a big risk of getting locked up if they suspect us."

"But what if the Arab soldiers think we are suspicious? Or what if we meet a patrol on the way, or some Arab peasants? You know good and well they never go without their daggers," Shalom objected uneasily.

Wild Man had even thought of that eventuality.

"If we meet Arab peasants, we'll just have to pretend that we are Arabs. We'll be dressed like they are, and we'll make our faces a little darker brown, and you, Shalom, you can speak Arabic and can talk with them if they ask us anything. As far as the soldiers are concerned, I think we'd better take some weapons with us. I've already had instruction here in the use of weapons—naturally, if the Arabs attack the kibbutz, we have to be able to defend ourselves against them."

"Arabs attack the kibbutz?" Shalom blurted out in surprise. "Could such a thing really happen?"

"Happen?" Wiseacre sneered. "Why do you suppose we have a watchtower right in the middle of the kibbutz? And why do you think there's a member of the kibbutz on guard duty there night and day? The tower was finished a year ago, and at that point we received weapons from the army. We're all border guards here," he added proudly, "in case you didn't know that before. All the members of the kibbutz, even the women, receive military training, and if the Arabs should attack us, every single one of us knows what his duty is on the defense team."

Shalom was more than a little astonished that he had never heard of this before and a little wounded that he hadn't yet had military training. But Wild Man cleared it all up by saying that only those who were fourteen years old took part in the defense operations of the kibbutz, while the youngest and the oldest members were supposed to take shelter in the strongest building of the kibbutz—the dining hall—in case of an Arab attack. "As soon as you're fourteen, I'm sure you'll get your military training, Shalom," Wild Man assured him. "At that point Moshe, the secretary, will take you in hand and teach you everything that the members of the kibbutz need to know." It came as a great surprise to Shalom to find out that Moshe had served as a captain in the Israeli Army during the War of Liberation, that Rudolf had been a lieutenant, and that most of the male members of the kibbutz had served in the army at that time. Even old Aunt Rosa, the supreme ruler of the kitchen nowadays, had been in charge of a first-aid station at the

Jerusalem front, and Sneaker's mother had been a messenger at one of the top headquarters.

After these explanations, Wild Man continued to point out why it was necessary to take weapons along on their cave expedition. He had decided that if they were surprised on the way, he could hold the attackers in check until the others had managed to get to safety. But where were they going to get weapons? That was the big question. It was Moshe who was responsible for rifles and machine guns, and these were stored together with the ammunition in a carefully locked weapon closet inside the office. Moshe's bed was also in the office, and even if he sometimes left the office during the day, his deputy Susanna, the bookkeeper and stenographer, was always there.

"Apart from the weapons in the closet, five members of the kibbutz have weapons," Sneaker reported. It was obvious that he had done a good deal of research on the subject. "They constitute a so-called alarm crew, and in case of an Arab attack they would have to go at once to their assigned positions in that part of the kibbutz that faces the border. This emergency group has been assigned weapons, and they carry them even when they're working in the fields."

"That may well be," Shalom interrupted, "but on Saturdays no one will be working. The thing we have to do is find out where the emergency squad keeps their weapons on Saturdays. If they keep them in their rooms, we might be able to get hold of a gun there somewhere."

They came to an agreement that next Saturday Sneaker would survey the situation in regard to the guns. And then Wild Man declared the meeting at an end. Out in the

chicken house the wide-awake roosters began to announce
the dawn for the faithful people of the kibbutz.

The next morning Rudolf found, to his astonishment, that
all desire to debate had suddenly left his four pupils and
that, instead of the steady stream of questions with which
they usually bombarded him, they sat quietly and sleepily
listening to his comments. Once in a while someone would
try to conceal an enormous yawn. Even the afternoon's work
was sluggish, in spite of the fact that all four of them had
been assigned to their favorite place—the dairy.

Kati wondered why it was that the boys had suddenly
become so frightened at the prospect of the cold nights that
they wanted their night shirts lengthened. Nevertheless, she
took the shirts and promised to lengthen them just the way
they wanted them. The boys thanked her effusively, much
more than she herself felt these small favors deserved.

In the days that followed, the boys made every effort to
be assigned duties that would enable all of them to be together. Rudolf noticed to what an extent the others had
accepted Shalom, and this made him happy. He didn't have
the slightest idea that the boys had cooked up a plan together and that it was this plan that had welded them together to such an unexpectedly high degree. Rudolf noticed
also that Shalom had suddenly begun to show an interest in
archaeology. At his request, Rudolf found the newspaper
article about the discoveries near the Dead Sea, and in addition he loaned him a book about archaeological excavations.
As was his habit, Shalom read the book in two days and
asked the following morning if it was possible that the
territory around the kibbutz might have been the hiding
place for any parchment scrolls or other archaeological
treasures.

A few days later it was Rudolf's turn to take guard duty in the tower in the afternoon, and Shalom begged to have an hour's release from work in order that he might pay him a visit up there. Once before he had been up in the tower, shortly after his arrival at the kibbutz, but on that occasion he displayed no great interest in the panorama that lay before him. Now he saw it all with new eyes and a completely different interest, especially the landscape off to the east. Rudolf showed him where the border was and let him use the binoculars, which gave him an opportunity to study carefully the sun-baked, barren grounds. Shalom decided that Wild Man had been right and had given a correct description of the terrain they would have to go through. Through the binoculars he saw the deep furrows of the wadi, followed by a flat stretch, a stony strip, and finally even the mouth of the huge cave in the long chain of mountains.

The following Saturday morning, Sneaker reported that the members of the emergency squad kept their guns in their bedrooms and went after them in the evenings when they were due to report for regular patrol duty. Thus it wouldn't be at all impossible to "appropriate" a gun in the middle of the day from a bedroom belonging to one of the emergency squad and to put it back before the evening meal. If everything went right, no one would ever notice the loan.

One afternoon when Wild Man was working in the warehouse, he discovered three short-handled spades—the kind soldiers usually use—and put them in a place where they could be easily gotten at if needed. That evening, they went over all the plans together carefully, and they were in agreement that the big adventure, or "excursion" as they themselves referred to it, should be attempted on the coming Saturday. "We probably don't dare wait any longer,"

Wiseacre pointed out, "because the rainy season will soon
set in, at which point the wadi will be full of rushing
waters."

The password was "next Saturday." The plans were complete, and there were a good many dreams of searching
through the cave and unearthing parchment scrolls and
other priceless finds.

In spite of their detailed preparations, however, there
was no "excursion." All of their plans collapsed on Wednesday when the workers of the kibbutz were out in the fields
gathering grapes. The grape clusters were ripe and round
among the dark green foliage; Moshe, the secretary, had,
the evening before, ordered all of them to start the harvest
the next day. Everyone was delighted, because the gathering of the grapes constituted a festival day when everyone
sang as they walked out to the fields and as they placed the
sweet grapes in their huge baskets. Eventually a cart came
out with an especially good meal from the kitchen, which
was eaten in the shade of the trees. In the evening there was
a harvest festival in the dining hall; there was music and
dancing. Moshe had even promised them some bottles of
wine for the harvest party; usually they had wine only on
the high holidays.

Early on Wednesday morning Moshe assigned the members of the kibbutz their various duties, as usual. Everyone
had crowded into the kibbutz's yard, and many of them were
already wearing the shoulder packs that would be used for
transporting the grapes. It was clear that everyone wanted to
take part in the harvest and that no one was inclined to drive
the cows to the pasture, which was quite a distance from the
vineyard. Embarrassed, Moshe scratched his ear. Certainly
he didn't want to deprive anyone of the joy of taking part

in the harvest. Rudolf saw through the situation immediately and offered himself to tend the cows that day.

"I'm very fond of animals," he said, "and I like to play herder. While the cows graze, I can read in peace and quiet. I've just received two new books through the mail, and this will be an excellent opportunity for me to leaf through them while I tend the cows."

Moshe gratefully accepted his offer, and a few minutes later the happy throng was on its way to the vineyard to begin the harvest. With a couple of books under his arm, a few sandwiches and a canteen of water in a sack slung over his back, and a gun over his shoulder, Rudolf drove the cattle from the barnyard out to pasture.

The work in the vineyard went along with great liveliness and joy. The food that was sent out from the kitchen tasted marvelous, and everyone was happily sure that this year's harvest was better than the previous year's had been. The baskets groaned under the weight of the clusters of grapes. But right in the middle of a song, gun fire was heard at a distance. Immediately they stopped singing, and everyone turned tensely in the direction from which the shot had come. Then everything was quiet again. The members of the emergency squad picked up the guns that they had laid aside within easy reach and, in accordance with Moshe's orders, hastened toward the watchtower. The voice of the secretary had a metallic clang as he cried out commandingly, "Women and children stay here and continue working. You men follow me."

Scarcely had he said this when a short series of gun shots could be heard coming from the watchtower, after which the deafening alarm signal could be heard. The men quickened their pace up the steps, women and children looked worriedly at one another, and a few little children began to cry. "The Arabs have attacked the kibbutz," said one of the women in a quaking voice.

Wild Man ran over to the other men, and Sneaker, Wiseacre, and Shalom remained quietly under one of the olive trees. Shalom would have preferred to join the men and accompany them to the central part of the kibbutz, but his sense of self-discipline won out over instinct, and he stayed with the others, following Moshe's instructions.

The next fifteen minutes were a time of nerve-racking waiting and uneasiness until Wild Man finally appeared on the path. It seemed like an eternity to Shalom before Wild Man came up to the group, all out of breath. But loudly enough for everyone to hear him, he proclaimed:

"Moshe has sent me back here to reassure you. It was just a small group of Arabs who had crossed the border, and when the guards fired at them from the watchtower, they fled from the field immediately. They took some cows from the pasture. That was all. There's not much chance of further attacks, and our people will soon be back here. Moshe has requested that everyone continue working just as if nothing had happened."

In the wake of these words of consolation, small groups got together and began to talk about the plundering Arabs and expressed regret over the cows they had lost. But soon these small groups broke up, and the harvest went on. But the gay atmosphere had gone, and no one seemed to be in the mood for singing. Now and then the women glanced toward the road to see if their husbands and sons would soon be back taking part in the work.

Even Wild Man picked out a vine and started to pick the ripe grapes, but his hands trembled nervously, and his basket had more leaves in it than grapes. The boys were gathered around him, wondering tensely if he had something additional to tell them. But Wild Man remained stubbornly silent until Sneaker asked him outright.

"It wasn't only the cows that the Arabs took," Wild Man said. "They took Rudolf, too. It was Rudolf who fired the first shot," he whispered. "The Arabs crawled on their stomachs clear up to the pasture, and that's why the guards in the tower didn't see them. . . . One of the Arabs was wounded in the foot by a machine-gun, and we captured him out in the meadow."

"Rudolf," the boys cried out in shock. Suddenly they realized how much affection they had for this man with the glasses, even though he corrected them so often during their morning lessons.

A few of the men had returned to the harvest work, and soon everyone knew what had happened. Once more all work ceased. The women were fearful of what might happen to Rudolf. The men said nothing, but the expressions on their faces were gloomy.

Farther down the road they could see a man running in their direction. It was the driver of the jeep—Avram. When he was still about fifty yards away, he began to shout.

"Shalom! Shalom, rush down to the office! Moshe is looking for you. He wants you right this minute."

Shalom couldn't imagine what the secretary wanted with him, but he began to speed toward the central part of the kibbutz. Outside the office, he was met by a man who led him into the sick room.

A rather young man in Arab clothing lay on a bed in the room. His eyes were closed, and there was a heavy bandage on one of his legs. Moshe stood beside the bed, together with one of the other men.

"Good thing you got here, Shalom," said Moshe. "This Arab got shot in the leg and had to stay behind out there in the pasture. We brought him here and tended his wound, and we gave him something to deaden his pain. Now I want to question him, and I want you to translate his answers. I can speak and understand a little Arabic, but you can make yourself understood much better than I can. First off, ask him what his name is and where he comes from."

14

The Genuine Adventure

More than an hour later Shalom wearily left the sick room. He had discovered that it wasn't entirely a simple matter to act as an interpreter and to question prisoners. His three friends were waiting for him outside the house, and Wild Man, in his usual fashion, commanded him to tell everything he had learned from the questioning of the Arab prisoner. Shalom made the excuse that he was terribly tired and added that Moshe would tell them about everything later on that evening. But Wild Man wasn't to be put off that easily.

"We don't have time to wait that long. I'm not asking out of curiosity. On the contrary, I have my own serious reasons. We have to liberate Rudolf . . ."

Naturally that made Shalom tell everything willingly. The Arab was from a village right on the border, but he was not in military service. He was a civilian. A patrol of eight men commanded by a lieutenant was stationed in the village, and the prisoner belonged to this patrol. Every day the lieutenant stationed himself somewhere on the mountain and observed the kibbutz through his telescope or binoculars, since, from his vantage point, he commanded an excellent view of the whole territory. The attack had been planned a long time back, and the Arab officer had trained ten civil-

ians from the village to take part in it. From the military
standpoint the attack had been aimed at blowing up the
kibbutz's watchtower and setting fire to the buildings, but
they had also promised the peasants that they would take the
Jews' cows as war trophies. That morning the lieutenant
had noticed that the kibbutz was deserted as everyone took
off to harvest the grapes in the vineyard, which was a good
distance from the watchtower. Accordingly, he gave an
immediate order for attack. The plan was that they would
crawl across the level strip and take the kibbutz by surprise.
They managed to remain concealed, reaching the pasture
land where Rudolf was tending the cows. According to the
plan, one of the soldiers was supposed to creep up behind
Rudolf, point a gun at him, and force him to give up. Another of the soldiers had an old rag ready to use as a gag and
a rope with which to bind Rudolf's hands behind his back.
But the calculations went awry. Either it was because the
soldier didn't approach noiselessly enough, or there was
something else that aroused Rudolf's attention. Whatever
the reason, he fired a shot from his gun before the Arab had
even gotten very close to him, and that was the shot the
people in the vineyard heard first.

The attackers were frightened by the shot, since they
hadn't counted on the fact that the herder of the kibbutz
would be tending the cows with a gun over his shoulder. But
one of the Arab soldiers managed to hit Rudolf in the neck
from behind and to wrestle the weapon from him. Immediately the lieutenant sent one of the soldiers back to the
Arab village with Rudolf in tow. Meanwhile, the Arab peasants drove the cows together in one place without bothering
to obey the lieutenant's instructions to wait until they had
had time to blow up the watchtower. Clearly, they were

much more interested in their trophies than they were in military strategy, and a good thing it was, too.

The shot from Rudolf's gun had made the guard in the watchtower aware that something was definitely wrong. Very soon he caught sight of the peasants who were chasing the cows and the soldiers who were tying Rudolf's arms behind his back, so he opened fire with the big machine gun. This was the short burst of shots the kibbutz members had heard from the vineyard. The machine gun fire notwithstanding, the lieutenant wanted to continue the attack, but the soldiers refused to obey him and went their own way. The Arab peasants were already on the way home to the village with the cows, and the lieutenant had no alternative but to follow their example. He advised the wounded man to try to crawl over the border, but the emergency squad of the kibbutz caught him before he made it.

"But what did the Arab say about Rudolf? Why did they drag him along with them instead of killing him on the spot as they usually do?" Wild Man questioned.

"The lieutenant had given his men strict orders to take at least one prisoner and had offered a reward to the one who could bring back a live Israeli. He had made clear to the soldiers that the military command in the nearest city wanted to capture a prisoner in order to question him about the Israeli border fortifications," Shalom answered, repeating word for word what the Arab prisoner had said.

Wild Man scratched his ear, coming eventually to the conclusion that, all other things being equal, Rudolf was surely still in the border village. Wiseacre agreed.

"The nearest city is about fifty miles from the village, and the road is in such poor condition that they couldn't make it there before the middle of the night, even if they had started right out from the village. And the Arabs are scared to death of the darkness. I'm positive that the lieutenant won't send Rudolf to the city before tomorrow morning."

"Well, in that case, we just have to cross the border this evening and free Rudolf," said Wild Man in a voice that invited no opposition. "Good thing that we had made preparations for an excursion," he added.

Right then and there they worked out a plan down to the last detail, assigning the various parts of the plan among themselves. Shalom wanted to take off that very moment, but Wild Man managed to talk him out of it.

"In the first place we have to wait until it gets dark. If we weren't here for supper, every single person in the kibbutz would know what we were up to, and Moshe might get it into his head to force us back. Let's eat as fast as we can and then meet outside the dormitory afterwards. And we'll leave the dining hall one by one so that we won't attract any special attention."

An hour and a half later the four boys were on their way to the border, dressed in their long nightshirts. Shalom saw that Wild Man, who led the procession, was holding a machine gun in his hands, ready to fire it. Although they had agreed before they set out that all talking would be strictly forbidden during the hike, Shalom couldn't help asking where he had gotten hold of the weapon.

"When the alarm sounded, weapons were passed out at the storehouse. Even I was given one. And when the danger had passed, I 'forgot' to turn mine back in. But we mustn't speak here . . ."

Soon they had arrived at the deep wadi, and Wild Man ordered a brief rest period in this natural hiding place. Suddenly Shalom thought of something and asked for permission to suggest a new plan.

"Well, why didn't you think of that earlier?" Wild Man snorted impatiently.

"I didn't know then that we were going to have a machine gun along with us," Shalom replied. "We've just got to change our plan of attack."

Hastily he set forth his new idea, and the three others realized immediately that he was absolutely right. They would have to make use of the electrifying effect of the machine gun to the best possible degree.

Out on the flat, open terrain on the other side of the wadi, they made their way with heightened caution, although there wasn't much risk that they would be discovered from that great a distance. The oncoming rainy season was already foreshadowed by the heavy clouds that concealed the moon, making the night almost pitch black. But they had to be scrupulously careful how they moved, for sounds carried very sharply in the hush of the night.

Soon they began to see the outlines of the cube-shaped houses in the Arab villages, clearly delineated against the dark sky. There too all lay in darkness. Electricity—a luxury that only the richest of the Arabs who lived in large cities could afford—had never come to the village. The darkness was broken by a single kerosene lamp deep in the shadows. And it was at the entrance to what was doubtless some sort of military station. The boys made their way across fields of dried corn stalks. The peasants had already gathered in the ears of corn, but they hadn't had time to collect the tall stalks, which they would use as winter fuel.

Wiseacre stationed himself in the corn field and took out a bottle of kerosene and a bunch of rags, all of which he had concealed under his nightshirt. With the machine gun in readiness, Wild Man headed off to the left, taking a wide swing around the houses, and assumed his position at the other side of the village. This did not consume any great amount of time, because the whole village consisted of no more than twenty houses, all built very close together as was the custom among the Arabs.

Sneaker headed toward the house farthest to the right, while Shalom, at least for the moment, stayed with Wiseacre, helping him to soak the rags in the kerosene. Suddenly the silence of the night was broken by ferocious barking—evidently someone's watchdog had caught the scent of strangers. Wiseacre and Shalom froze in their tracks when they heard the noise, fearful that the dog might awaken the entire village. But they hardly had time to be really frightened, because all of a sudden a volley of machine-gun shots was heard from the other side of the village.

This was the sign for Wiseacre and Shalom to go into action. With no hesitation, Shalom took off toward the only street in the village, the entrance to which was no more than two hundred yards from where they stood. A few seconds later Wiseacre struck a match and began to set fire to the kerosene-soaked rags, which he had distributed among the corn stalks. They were so dry that they burned like tinder, and before Shalom had gotten to the first house, the fire had spread ten or fifteen yards farther into the corn field and was getting larger by the minute.

From behind the house to the right came a great commotion, which sounded very much like a salvo of machine guns. "That's Sneaker going to town with the rattles," Shalom mused contentedly as he leaned expectantly against the wall of the house. The rattles were used in the orange groves to scare birds who were always pecking holes in the orange skins and feasting on the sweet, juicy fruit. All the while the fruit was ripening, the rattles sounded night and day in the groves in order to keep away the unwelcome guests. It was Wiseacre who had suggested that they take the rattles with them on their "excursion."

More machine-gun shots followed, but from another part of the village than had happened earlier. In line with their plan, Shalom now began to shout at the top of his lungs, in Arabic, "Help! Help! The Jews have attacked the village."

A few seconds later the whole village was in panic. The dazed peasants—men, women, and children—rushed out of their houses to see what was going on. The fire, Shalom's desperate cry for help, the rattles, and the shots from the machine gun stirred them up to such an extent that they began to scream and rush headlong down the street. The confusion mounted and reached an absolute climax when the soldiers put in their appearance. With nothing but his pants on, the lieutenant stood, shouting commands to his soldiers, who were rashly heading off in the direction of the fire. The lieutenant strode into his quarters and returned with a revolver in his hand. Blindly he fired several shots into the air and then ran to join his subordinates. A few screaming women took off after him. Wild Man let a few more shots go, and the Arabs who were still in the street fled breathlessly into their houses.

Shalom and Wiseacre helped to create additional chaos by bellowing as loudly as possible, while Sneaker was manning the rattles close to the walls of the houses. Shalom, rushing over to the lighted entrance, found no one there and hurried in. He was right. It was the soldiers' quarters—a combined dormitory and guard house. It was dark inside, but he could make out a desk to the left, beyond which was a small annex—obviously the lieutenant's room. The room just opposite seemed to be empty, and the straw strewn over the floor revealed that it must be the dormitory for the enlisted men. The two rooms were separated by a narrow corridor, at the far end of which was a door, barricaded by a crossbar, which meant that it couldn't be opened from the other side. It didn't take Shalom a moment to lift the crossbar and open the door, which led to a small windowless cubicle. Feeling around with his hands, he soon bumped into a body down in one corner.

"Rudolf," he whispered. "Is it you?"

The reply came in the form of a groan. Finding some matches in his pocket, Shalom lit one and discovered that it really was Rudolf lying there. There was a gag around his mouth, and he was bound hand and foot; he could neither speak nor move. At this point the scout knife that Shalom had gotten as a present from Wild Man came into play. It took a little while before Shalom was able to cut the heavy rope, and still more time passed before Rudolf could stand on his benumbed legs.

They could hear a hollow clatter from the street, which made Rudolf come to a sudden stop in the corridor. But Shalom wasn't frightened because he knew that it was only the sound of the cows who had been let out of the enclosure. Sneaker and Wiseacre were supposed to take advantage of the general panic to find the cows in the enclosure, cut the ropes that held them, and drive them out onto the street. Everything had gone as planned, Shalom decided, for at least twenty cows came rushing out into the street, stirring up a huge cloud of dust.

It was no easy matter for Shalom to take care of Rudolf, who was minus his glasses. Also, his legs were stiff and numb from the ropes. Shalom almost had to drag him, and he was perspiring heavily before they made it past the last house in the village. The plan then was that they would head to the right of the burning corn field and continue on until they came to the small elevation in the terrain, which was their agreed-upon meeting place. Rudolf had regained his powers of locomotion and was once again able to run. And a lucky thing it was, too, because scarcely had they gotten to the outskirts of the village when they heard two sharp shots and the usual whistling sounds that ensue. Obviously the lieutenant had returned to the village and discovered that his prisoner had been freed. Shalom was quite sure that one of the bullets had whizzed past his ear, and in his fright he quickened his pace. He had covered a distance of about ten yards when he turned around, only to find that Rudolf was standing still, moaning faintly. Shalom at once went back to join him.

"I've been shot in the arm," Rudolf said gloomily.

Shalom grabbed hold of Rudolf's shirt and began to drag him along. The wound was obviously painful, and this, in combination with the fact that he was already weak from having been tied up, brought him almost to the point of fainting. The next time Shalom turned around, he saw, to his horror, that the lieutenant was running in their direction with a revolver in his hand. Just a few minutes more, he thought, and we'll both be prisoners.

Their enemy couldn't have been more than thirty yards from them when Wild Man's gun again went into action

from over by the small hill. In the light of the burning field, the upper part of the Arab's body could be seen clearly, and he made an excellent target. Still, he was not hit. The distance was too great for Wild Man to aim perfectly. But this was a soldier, and he knew that his only chance of saving himself was to fall flat on the ground, which action gave Shalom and Rudolf the small head start they needed.

On the small hill Wild Man, Wiseacre, and Sneaker were excitedly awaiting their arrival. Sneaker's long shirt was as soiled and dirty as if he had taken a bath in the dust of the road, and his nose was bleeding slightly. Pressing an equally dirty handkerchief to his face, he swore softly to himself.

"Are you wounded, too?" Shalom asked in fright.

"Naah! It was only one of those stupid cows that knocked me over backwards, and I fell and hit my nose . . ."

This was no time for idle chatter. Wild Man immediately gave the order to retreat. Rudolf and Sneaker led the procession, and Wild Man brought up the rear. Now and again he glanced behind to see if they were being followed, but he could see no one. Finally—after what seemed an eternity to Shalom, they came to the deep bed of the wadi.

Rudolf's arm was bleeding badly; his face seemed as pale as the faint moon. On the spur of the moment, Wild Man tore off one of his shirt sleeves and improvised a tourniquet for the wound. Shalom and Wiseacre put their arms around Rudolf's waist and assisted him. This was no easy matter, because Rudolf was heavy, but they might never make it otherwise.

"Halt! Who goes there?" a military voice suddenly shouted to the little group.

"Your own people," Shalom shouted in delight, since the order had been spoken in Hebrew.

They had made it to the border. They were safe. The minute the guard on the watchtower had reported an exchange of shots and the glow of the fire on the other side of the border, the armed men of the kibbutz had headed for the wadi with their weapons in hand. They had no idea of what was going on over there, but they felt it was best to be on their guard.

Cautiously, Shalom and Wiseacre lowered the exhausted Rudolf to the ground, while Wild Man gave a very military sort of report to Moshe, who had meanwhile arrived at the scene.

"Mission accomplished with success. Four unhurt, one wounded."

"Excellent, thank you," said Moshe, strictly according to regulations, but added in his "civilian" voice, "We'll talk further about this mission tomorrow. Now I want two of you guards to carry Rudolf into the office, and be careful how you handle him."

The next morning three military jeeps drove up in front of the office building. Several officers climbed out and hurried into the office, where Moshe was waiting for them. The military commission, led by a captain, had come to establish protocol in connection with the Arab attack of the previous day and to take the Arab prisoner to the military command post in the city.

But the military commission had more to do than it had expected. They had to establish protocol not only in connection with the Arab attack, but also in connection with Rudolf's liberation and the "mission" in general. And not only the Arab, but also Rudolf, had to be placed in the ambulance jeep. A quarter of an hour later, both wounded men were on their way to the city, where they were to be given medical attention. Before their departure, a member of the hospital corps had examined Rudolf's wound and declared, to the relief of everyone, that the bullet had probably not damaged the bone structure and that it was undoubtedly just a flesh wound.

The members of the night "mission" were now assembled outside the office, waiting to be questioned. Wild Man was whistling absent-mindedly. Now and then Sneaker felt his swollen nose, and Wiseacre spent the whole time explaining that they would never be punished for crossing the border illegally when the results of their accomplishment were taken into consideration. Shalom didn't quite know what to think about the whole matter. At breakfast, Moshe had dutifully lectured all four of them, saying that the first duty of a soldier was to be disciplined and not to obey the impulse of the moment. The members of the kibbutz, on the other hand, had hugged and kissed them, which had embarrassed Shalom slightly, especially when Kati was the one doing the hugging.

Finally the office door opened, and Moshe motioned to the boys to come in. The captain of the military command sat at the desk. Over his left eye he wore a black patch. There were five rows of multicolored ribbons on his uniform. Shalom recalled having seen his picture in the newspapers now and then. He was one of the great heroes of the War of Liberation, and he had lost his left eye in a night attack.

Over by the wall, where Moshe's stenographer usually sat, were two young officers taking careful note of everything that was said during the period of questioning. The four boys were lined up in front of the desk, and the captain subjected them to a regular inquisition. To begin with, Wild

Man had to report, down to the last detail, on the preparations for the archaeological excursion they had earlier planned and on the actual mission that accomplished the liberation of Rudolf. Wild Man spoke calmly and guardedly, but he kept nothing from them—not even the fact that it was he who had been the ringleader. From time to time the captain interrupted him with a question. His dry voice was anything but an omen of mercy. Downcast, Shalom stood there wondering what punishment they would get.

"And what actually did you have in mind when you risked the wrath of an entire Arab village, where there are military garrisons and a number of armed citizens, with just a single machine gun?" the one-eyed man asked Wild Man.

"Well, Rudolf had told us that during the War of Liberation, he had seen countless signs indicating that the Arabs were terrified of night fighting and that they were easily panicked," Wild Man replied.

"And why did you turn the cows loose? Whose idea was that?" came the next question.

Wiseacre stepped out of line and in a trembling voice admitted that he had been the one to suggest the idea. He had counted on the fact that if he could only let them loose, they would surely find their way back home to the kibbutz.

"I thought of how hard we had had to work to get the money to buy the cows. I didn't want us to lose them. And for that matter, it helped to create more panicky confusion among the Arabs as the cows wandered along the street," he explained.

"One of them knocked me over," Sneaker interjected angrily, making the young officers break into laughter. A glance from the captain made quick work of their enjoyment.

At this point Moshe asked to say a few words, and he told the captain that during the night seven cows had come back to the kibbutz from the other side of the border.

"I knew that they'd come back if only I could get them loose," said Wiseacre triumphantly. "I'm the top specialist on cows among the four of us," he said with ill-concealed pride.

The captain now began to question Shalom, and his questions seemed to pierce the air as Wild Man's shots had the night before.

"And how does it happen that you speak Arabic so well? Was it your idea to get your nightshirts lengthened? Weren't you afraid to go into their quarters? Didn't it occur to you that some of the soldiers might still be inside?"

Suddenly Shalom felt exasperated and defiant, especially since he thought that the one-eyed officer was being harder on him than he had been on the others. As a result, he answered all the questions without evasion, but hastily and angrily. At the end, he added in a low voice, "And for another thing, if we hadn't gone across the border, Rudolf, if he were still alive, would be sitting somewhere in an Arab jail right this minute."

"And we wouldn't have gotten the cows back, either," Wiseacre added.

The captain silenced them both and said emphatically:

"In the old Austro-Hungarian Army, there is a high decoration that is called 'The Order of Maria Theresa.' It is handed out to those soldiers who, without orders, or in direct opposition to orders, take independent action against their enemies. If their missions go well, they receive the order; if they fail, they are punished for breach of discipline. The Israeli Army has no such order, but we do hand out punishment to undisciplined soldiers who take things into their own hands. Have I made myself clear?"

"But we're not soldiers," objected Wiseacre.

"Silence! As citizens of this small country, with enemies everywhere around us, all of us are soldiers. Even you. Is that clear?"

His words made Shalom even more angry, and in a spirit of reckless abandon, which afterwards he was scarcely able to understand, he barked at the captain, "Well, then, if I'm a soldier, I want to do my military service with the fliers. I want to be in the Air Corps . . ."

A small smile appeared on the captain's face. The voice in which he spoke was in direct contrast to the voice he had been using all along.

"I'll remember that, my boy. And you other three," he said to the other boys, "will be the guests of the army in about two weeks. As my own personal adjutants, you'll take part in the autumn maneuvers. Gentlemen, the protocol business is over. The matter is closed."

A Postscript

A couple of years ago, the author of this book was sent by his newspaper on a trip to the Middle East. It all started with a flight on a Scandinavian Airlines plane to Athens, and from there, when an article on Greece had been completed, the journey continued on to Istanbul, the old and beautiful capital city of the Turkish Sultans. The third stop was to be Israel. At the Yesilköy airport in Istanbul was an El Al Israel plane ready for departure.

The day was brilliantly sunny, and the DC-6 took off from the airport, flying in a cloudless sky over the high, rocky mountains of Asia Minor. After a flight time of an hour and a half, the nine-thousand-foot mountain Ak Dag could be seen off to the right, its snowy peak glistening in the blinding sunlight. Soon the azure blue waves of the Mediterranean spread out below, and the five passengers in the plane had every reason to feel that the trip would be unusually pleasant.

According to the timetable, the El Al plane, before swinging off to the southeast, was to fly over Cyprus, continuing then with its passengers to the Lod airport in Tel Aviv. But the weather began to play tricks with the timetable, which ultimately had to be changed completely. A few miles after we had left the Turkish coast behind us, dark clouds suddenly appeared, causing the pilot to gain altitude in an attempt to escape the threatening storm. But the storm clouds were obviously heavier than he had counted on, even at the higher altitude. The DC-6 groped about in what seemed to be miles and miles of solid cotton-batting. It grew dark in the plane, and a thick mist hung just outside the double oval windows. The quiet flight became rougher and rougher.

In no time at all the sign "Fasten Safety Belts" lighted up. The "No Smoking" sign soon followed. The pleasant stewardess hurried into the pilot's cabin and shortly thereafter informed us over the microphone that a huge storm was reported over the eastern half of the Mediterranean and that the plane had been instructed to land at the airport in Nicosia, the capital of Cyprus, and to wait there until the storm had passed.

The airport at Nicosia could not by any stretch of the imagination be called luxurious or modern, especially with reference to the waiting rooms and the general comfort of the passengers. The terminal building consisted only of a huge wooden barracks with a cement floor. At some point during World War II, it had been constructed by the British Royal Air Force.

The five passengers from the El Al plane, plus its personnel, sat at the counter in the waiting room, talking and drinking orange juice. The heavy rains of the subtropical storm laid a misty veil over the runway.

For lack of other diversion, I took out my portable typewriter and began to write my report on Turkey. My fellow passengers, two Israeli businessmen, an elderly lady, and a Turkish diplomat, didn't strike me as especially interesting. Suddenly I found myself unable to take my eyes off one of the pilots—a thin young man of medium height, with unusually delicate, narrow hands and long, pointed fingers. But what caught my attention especially were his dark-skinned, oval-shaped face and his huge black eyes. His short hair was almost jet black. "A genuine oriental face in the best sense of the term. A fine example of an ancient, refined race," I said to myself.

Conversation with the young man in the elegant dark-blue pilot's uniform seemed to spring up almost of itself, and I asked him without any hesitation where he came from.

"I'm an Israeli, but I was born in Yemen," the copilot answered with a smile.

Yemen—that mysterious country with a community life that had never progressed beyond the Middle Ages. To a foreigner the country had always seemed hermetically sealed off from the rest of the world. It had always sparked my journalistic imagination. The copilot answered all my questions openly, always with a friendly, sympathetic smile. We sat there talking for almost a whole hour, and I found him so pleasant that I scarcely noticed the rain had stopped almost as suddenly as it had begun. The captain hurried over to the control tower, returning a few minutes later with good news.

"The storm is over. Please return to the plane. We are leaving immediately for Tel Aviv."

My new-found friend with the sparkling white teeth and the dark face got up and headed for his place on the flight deck. But before we said good-by to one another, he handed me his card and invited me to look him up some time in Israel. The address on the card was Ramat Gan, Hanegev Street 11.

All the way from Nicosia to Tel Aviv, we were blessed with clear skies, and as I left the plane, I saw that the copilot was being met at the exit by a beautiful young lady with chestnut-brown hair and large, gray eyes.

Four days later, a Saturday according to the calendar in the reception room of the hotel—the Sabbath, when all business offices, editorial offices, and shops would be closed —I puzzled over my breakfast coffee, wondering what to do with my free day. All of a sudden, I recalled the El Al copilot. I took out his card and called him up. I was in luck. He was free that day and assured me that I was very welcome to come to his home for coffee after lunch.

A beautiful green lawn surrounded the small three-room villa in Ramat Gan, a suburb characterized by sand dunes and a view of the blue sea. A hedge of azaleas in full bloom led up to the front door. A polished brass sign on the gate announced to the world that Shalom Mizrachi lived there.

In the living room, where the curtains had been drawn to shut out the heat of the sun, I was introduced to Shalom's wife, Katrine—the young lady I had seen at the airport. Our conversation went on far into the evening, and I was invited to stay for dinner.

The events I have described in my book are those that were told to me in the little villa in Ramat Gan with its oriental draperies and its modern furniture.

The story of Shalom's life would not be complete without saying that the one-eyed captain, who in time became the Commander-in-Chief of the Israeli Army, kept his promise. A few weeks after the inquisition in the office of the kibbutz, Shalom was summoned to the Nahal command. Nahal is a sort of war college, where the pupils also engage in farm work in their free time.

After spending four years in Nahal, Shalom was accepted in the training school of the Air Corps, and in 1956

he took part in the Suez campaign with the rank of an en-
sign. He served as a radio officer on an ambulance plane.

He and Kati had been married for two years when he
took a job with El Al following his discharge from the
service. They were expecting their first baby, and Shalom
was hoping that it would be a boy.

The other people in the story are still in Israel. Mori
Alfeka has departed this life. Rudolf is a professor at the
Hebrew University in Jerusalem, Wiseacre is studying veteri-
nary medicine, Sneaker has made the grade as a famous
soccer player, and last year Wild Man was elected the
secretary of the kibbutz.

It was very late when I at last said good-by to Shalom
and Kati Mizrachi. Far off in the starry night I could hear
the sound of an airplane and see its white lights blinking
from the wings.